RICHARD ALLEN
SKINHEAD ESCAPES

Richard Allen was the pen-name of James Moffat, born in Canada in 1922.

Moffat was prolific, though one repeated claim that he was the author of 'at least 290 novels in several genres under at least 45 pseudonyms' still requires independent verification. It is known that Moffat contributed to an early draft of the novel *Somewhere in The Night*, which was later completed (or entirely rewritten – sources differ) by Michael Moorcock and published under the pseudonym Bill Barclay in 1966.

However it was Moffat's gritty youthsploitation novels, all written in the 1970's under the name Richard Allen, that form the bulk of his legacy today. The Joe Hawkins story began in *Skinhead* (1970) and was continued in *Suedehead* (1971). Later there were further instalments in Joe Hawkins' story, as well as novels focussing on other youth movements such as *Smoothies* (1973), *Punk Rock* (1977) and the final Allen novel *Mod Rule* (1980). Altogether there were eighteen novels under the Richard Allen brand.

James Moffat spent most of his final decade in obscurity, though he lived to see the reissue of the Richard Allen novels in the early 1990's. He died in July of 1993, while living in a nursing home in Newton Abbot.

RICHARD ALLEN

SKINHEAD ESCAPES

DEAN STREET PRESS

Published by Dean Street Press 2016

Copyright © 1972 Richard Allen

All Rights Reserved

Published by licence, issued under the UK Orphan Works
Licensing Scheme

First published in 1972 by New English Library

Cover by DSP

ISBN 978 1 911579 47 2

www.deanstreetpress.co.uk

AUTHOR'S NOTE

Judging by the popularity of the paperbacks, *Skinhead* and *Suedehead*, the pundits are totally wrong when they state that teenage cultism is fading away. It would appear, from the response to *Suedehead*, that skinheads are like old soldiers – they are forever there in the wings.

After two books featuring Joe Hawkins, it was my intention to let the character rest for an indeterminate period of time. The readers, however, have decided otherwise. Letters from the book-buying public make it patently clear that Joe is an established favourite. Almost without exception, these letters request – no, *insist*– on another Joe book. Whilst it is exceedingly gratifying for an author to find his works included in the top ten paperbacks of the year, it poses certain problems to meet the demands.

Joe, we remember, found himself confronted with a four-year prison sentence in *Suedehead*. That seemed, to me, to put paid to his activities for quite a while. But Joe Hawkins is a resourceful character. An old adage mentions not being able to keep a good man down. The same holds true for the Joes of this world. Bad pennies, like good men, have a habit of turning up at an alarming speed.

In years to come, Joe Hawkins will probably be quoted as an example of this era we have named "the permissive age". If so, then the author can count on more than sales success. With that thought in mind, I wish to thank all those who have spread the gospel and taken the trouble to write. It is for you that *Skinhead Escapes* is specially written.

Richard Allen, *Gloucester, 1972.*

CHAPTER ONE

From his cell window, Joe Hawkins could see the high wall forming one side of their rectangle exercise yard. Beyond it, he knew, were a few scattered cottages belonging to the prison staff with neat, cared-for gardens reaching down to a small stream and the woods that filled his horizon. This morning, he could not see past the wall. In fact, it was getting so bleeding misty he was having difficulty making out the worn, pocked bricks of the wall.

He smiled at the thoughts the all-embracing mist brought in its chilling, clammy wake. If only he was in a working party with permission to go outside the bloody prison! Man, he wouldn't waste a single precious second lingering with doubts in his mind. He'd make a break for the wide open spaces and freedom.

The sounds of pot-carriers brought him back to reality. It was an indignity forcing men to carry their covered pots through seemingly endless corridors and empty the rotten things in a communal latrine. There was no valid necessity for this outdated duty. None except the Victorian concept that prisoners should be treated like so many animals.

He was still mentally tearing the system apart when they went outside. He was glad he had a three-quarters length coat to wear. The weather had turned nasty. He saw other prisoners in their lightweight jackets slapping arms round their chests to keep out the insidious fog. All right for them, he thought viciously. When this lark is over they'll go indoors to semi-warmth. I've bleedin' got to clean up this rotten yard.

Angling across the tendril-deep yard he joined a group wearing coats like his. A grim-featured warder scowled at him, silently motioning at a stack of brooms. The others watched with expressions Joe found difficult to describe. Something was wrong. He sensed it. There was just a prison feeling in the air that "spoke" of conspiracy. He grabbed a broom and moved to one side. The last thing he wanted was to become involved in a kangaroo court punishment.

The mist swirled round them. A whistle blew and the great mass of prisoners began to form into lines. Exercise, for this day, had ended.

"Keep your nose out of what happens, Hawkins," a gruff voice said in Joe's ear.

The man looked straight ahead, broom making sweeping gestures without accomplishing much in the way of cleanliness. Joe recognised him, and a sudden tremor of anticipation raced through his body. He'd been wrong about this being some sort of convict court execution. He knew what was going to happen as surely as if he had been in on the plan from the beginning.

"I'm going with you, McVey!"

Cold snake-eyes bored into Joe. "Try it, kid. Try it an' you're dead!"

Joe forced a grin. He saw the warder sidestep a broom and lean against the moist running wall. "I won't hinder you – I promise."

"Damned right you won't," the heavy man snarled with mounting anger.

"Turn it up, Charlie." The speaker drifted between McVey and Joe, glaring at the unwanted intruder as he did. "Get lost, Hawkins!"

"I'm going with you," Joe whispered.

A broom handle slammed into Joe's gut, sending him reeling. A wave of nausea washed over him and it was all he could do to maintain his balance. Tears stung his eyes.

"I'm going," Joe said through tight lips.

McVey smiled, and told his companion, "He's got us, Len."

"Gutsy," the other allowed.

"Pity to kill the bastard," McVey remarked.

Joe felt terror crawl through every nerve-end. These men did not joke about such things. Killing him would be no more on their conscience than him killing a spider.

"Ten minutes from now," the man Len said. "Other side of the yard." He straightened and faced Joe. "You've been warned, kid." He started sweeping, crossing the damp yard without pause, deliberately coming between McVey and the frowning warder.

"Sorry, Hawkins. There's no room for an extra passenger." McVey actually appeared to feel something in that brief moment.

Joe leant on his broom, his stomach hurting. Whatever they said he fully intended to make the break with them. He loathed prison, the years that stretched ahead of him behind grey walls. He would have to take a chance and, once outside, evade their clutches. They wouldn't stop him during the actual break-out. That would be risking too much.

"You're not 'ere for your 'olidays, me lad," the warder bellowed. His large feet sounded ominous as he walked across the cobbled yard to stand over Joe. "Are you sick?" The face looked anxious as his eyes searched Joe's features.

"No, Mister Simpson."

"Then sweep!"

Joe worked furiously, conscious of the warder's gaze and the ache in the pit of his stomach. That bloody broom handle had hurt. He owed the bastard Len one.

Somewhere on the other side of the wall a car engine roared into life. A figure appeared on top of the wall – ghostly as mist clung to it. A rope ladder snaked down into the yard and smacked the cobblestones with a dull thud.

Simpson, huge feet sounding on the wet stone, slid to a halt, mouth hanging open as he stared upwards in amazement. Before he could raise an alarm, McVey brought his broom down on the man's head with a crashing sound of splintering wooden handle and cracking bone. Simpson toppled and lay still.

Joe wanted to drop to his knees to examine the felled warder. He had not counted on murder being part of the plan. Now he had a momentary doubt about joining the mass exodus – but only momentary.

Six men weaved as the rope ladder swung wildly, hands and feet fighting to retain their precious hold on the precarious escape hope. Joe jumped forward, unaware that he still clutched his broom.

"Not you, kid!"

Joe skidded to a stop. Len stood at the foot of the ladder, knife in one hand, eyes slitted. *If only I had my bovver boots*, Joe thought and automatically used the only weapon within range – his broom. Len wasn't prepared for this strange kid coming at him. If he had taken time to acquaint himself with

Joe's record he might have been more inclined to treat the youth as an equal in viciousness. But he hadn't. And that was his downfall!

The broom reversed with a swiftness that caught Len totally immobile. Only as the rounded, unyielding butt end speared at his face did the crook try to duck. Too late. Joe felt the shock travel along his forearms, saw the man's lips split and blood spurt. He heard the telltale crunch of bone and teeth hung loose amid the destruction of Len's features. Nothing daunted, Joe brandished the broom again, bringing it crossways onto the man's nose. Len sagged, knife falling from hand. Dropping his broom, Joe slashed at the other's groin with his hard prison-issue boot, spat at the stricken victim of another aggro, and vaulted onto the rope ladder.

He was agile, a monkey climbing a tree. He arrived breathing easily on the wall as McVey's head was disappearing down the outside. Their eyes clashed and, in that instant, Joe realised he could never reach the ground with his fellow-escapers and stay intact. Down below, like some gigantic monster from Earth's dark past, a moving van waited in the mist. Judging the distance as best he could, Joe leaped into space . . .

CHAPTER TWO

Condensation trickled down the inside panes of the tall window. On a coffee table beside an expensive, antique sofa a national newspaper lay neatly folded across the middle. With some difficulty, Joe managed to make out the splash headline.

4 ESCAPEES RECAPTURED

Shivering as rain beat a mysterious drumming on the foliage surrounding the house, Joe cursed his lousy luck. His ankle hurt something awful. It was swollen, throbbing like a bad toothache. He knew to remove his boot would be fatal. Yet, he wanted to rub the bruised bone, the puffed flesh.

God, he thought. *I've got to find some grub!*

He pondered the advisability of breaking into the house and kicked the idea out almost immediately. A man entered the enormous room, went directly to the newspaper and opened it. Where the condensation formed irregular patterns on the glass the man's face floated in absurd contortions — wavering, twisting, shapeless often, forming anew into a picture of country squire the next. Not a man to tackle in his condition, Joe allowed. Probably an ex-army officer with more than a little unarmed combat experience. The type to clear steer of right then.

Limping away from the house, Joe slunk through woods to the cottage he had skirted earlier. It seemed like months since the jail break. He was so bloody cold and hungry. So unsure of this green, spacious nowhere. Give him the concrete pavements, the belching exhaust fumes, the warren of streets with their hiding places and dolly birds willing to feed and shelter a man for a few quick feels.

The cottage looked empty. He approached a window cautiously. After what he had gone through he did not want his freedom to end right here. Peering inside, he saw dust sheets covering indistinct furniture. He went to another window. The same scene greeted his gaze. He tried the window. Locked, doubly secured with spikes driven through both frames. He swore mentally, then went to the rear door. Testing it, he felt it give. He rubbed rain and dirt from the upper glass. One Yale-type lock and a bolt. A bloody large bolt.

He wrapped a soiled, wet handkerchief round his fist and drove the glass pane in. Carefully removing jagged shards, he reached inside, undid bolt and lock and swung the door open.

A mouse squeaked as it ran for cover. He plodded across a large farmhouse style kitchen to cupboards filling one entire wall. He opened them eagerly. Tins lined the lower shelves, sacks of sugar and flour the upper ones, packets of biscuits and cake mixes a corner area.

His hand hesitated near the tinned foods. Beans? Cocktail sausages? Spaghetti rings? Pineapple chunks? Bully beef? Chilli con Carne? *(What the hell was that?)* King crab? Shrimps? Chicken Gumbo soup? Lobster Bisque soup? Tuna?

Wolf-like, he tore at the key of the bully beef tin and opened it. As he swallowed hunks wholesale he found a wall-bracket can opener and removed the tops of shrimps and beans. With that inside him he felt better. But still ravenous. He needed tea and bread. The refrigerator was empty and disconnected. The gas stove had been turned off at the main. The bread bin was spotless; empty, too.

Rain slashed into the kitchen and he closed the door. No sense asking for some nosey bastard poking his head in where it wasn't wanted!

He searched the cottage from bottom to top. In one bedroom he discovered decent clothing. He changed from his wet prison gear and dried himself in the bathroom. He enjoyed the feel of clean underwear against his skin even although it was just a shade too large for him. It didn't matter about the bulk-knit sweater, though. Nor the faded slacks. Tucked inside the pair of gum-boots he had noticed he would be like many another local farming clod. There was an old hat, raincoat. He studied himself in a mirror. Nobody would ever take him for an East Ender. He felt satisfied, still hungry . . .

An hour had passed now since he broke into the cottage. A heap of opened, empty tins littered the kitchen table. His belly rumbled from being over-stuffed. His ankle hurt worse than ever although the torn sheet binding it helped considerably. At least, he mused, he hadn't broken the bloody thing!

He considered the telephone in the lounge. Dare he make a call to London? He gave up the notion. If this place was on a manual exchange his goose would really be cooked.

He smiled. His thinking machine was working in top gear. Native cunning had its good points. Those stupid bastards getting caught would curse him but he didn't care. He had outsmarted all of them.

The rain was easing off. He would have to move along. God knows how far he was from civilisation, from London. He did not relish the prospect of travelling in daylight yet he had no choice. Hanging around this cottage was an invitation for that army character to take a walk and find him. Whatever he did, distance had to be put between the cottage and Joe Hawkins before the police got a description of the missing clothing. As it was, he was too close to the prison yet for comfort. He could have covered a greater mileage if only he had managed to keep his footing on that moving van's roof.

He could still see those startled faces peering upwards as he careered off the greasy roof and landed in fall-breaking bushes. Luckily, surprise had been with him. Before the others could apprehend him he had limped off into the swallowing mist and vanished from their sight. It hadn't been easy getting away. But for the fact that the authorities had been chasing the van he could never had made good his lone escape.

What he needed most was money. And cigarettes. After that he would play it cool until the heat lifted . . .

*

Lottie Newman lived alone with her dreams. At twenty-three she did not classify herself as one of those on-the-shelf women without hope of ever snaring a husband. She could, if she wished, have her pick from a dozen or more eligible males. Modesty, and a desire to be completely honest with herself prevented her from calling the mirrored image confronting her beautiful. She was pretty, and shapely. That sufficed for a personal examination. When she decided the time was right for picking a husband she would pick carefully, security being the uppermost consideration. She did not go for having a handsome man about the house, nor one addicted to giving her a good time on dates. She preferred to know that there was money in the bank and a roof over her head which neither loan company nor mortgage society could ever take away. These things were paramount.

She turned slightly, posturing. The green velvet dress held against her nudity did something for her blonde hair, her bright green eyes. It also did more than something for her pert, thrusting breasts when draped round her slender figure.

Smiling, she threw the dress aside and raced hands lightly down her smooth flanks. She was an unabashed sensualist. At night, when reality subtly changed into erotic dreamland, she forgot security and concentrated on the pleasures of her flesh. She was not a prude although there was never any suggestion she was a permissive slut, either. She had been to bed with men and enjoyed the ecstasy of mutually sponsored gratification. The Pill was a boom when the mood for intercourse filled her being with uncontrollable longing.

Like now!

Shaking out her long blonde hair she swung towards the window. What she wouldn't give at that moment for a man to come into view and see her nakedness. *God, I'm a perverted bitch*, she thought happily. Standing in a doorway kitty-corner from her window she saw the man. Or was it a boy? She bent forward, her breasts pressed against the cold glass.

A shiver approaching orgasm flooded her loins. She could see those narrowed eyes gazing upwards, devouring her body. Suddenly, she retreated – ashamed. What must he think of her? She was behaving like a common prostitute advertising her professional ability. She blushed and hurriedly slipped into the velvet dress. The mood had vaporised. She was back to semi-normality . . .

*

What a bird! Joe thought as he strained to catch another glimpse of that lush nudity. His situation was desperate yet the need for a woman's hands on him, the touch of silken thighs slowly widening, was every bit as strong within his mind as getting loot.

A green dress moved across the curtained window. She had covered herself! Bitch!

Cold, unrelenting rain fell, bouncing off the lonely street. The doorway wasn't deep enough to prevent some wetting his trousers. He bent, tucking them inside his gum-boots. To hell with what these hick townspeople thought of a country yokel. His comfort was more important than the opinions of a few thousand idiots.

He had never heard of Kidderminster before and never wanted to see it again. The town was dying on its feet. Empty shops and rubbish-littered pavements reminded him of Plaistow and the degree of poverty one found there. From the huge signs outside some of the factories he knew they made carpets here. All he could say to that was "people are covering their floors with newspapers these days".

If the number of cars parked in the factories' parking lots was any criterion they were working at half capacity.

Congratulating himself on his perspicacity, Joe began to wonder about the girl. She had looked like a decent sort. Not the usual run of whore. Yet, what was she doing showing her natural beauty and living in a dump like this?

The house opposite was old, sadly in need of paint and new guttering. Rain splashed from the roof in cascades, racing down stained walls, flooding over a small canopy which barely managed to keep steps dry. He could see nameplates on the door. He grinned, trying to figure which room she occupied and darted across the street.

Why not? he asked himself. *Why not indeed?*

The names were written in a spidery scrawl. Mr & Mrs Vernon. Jonathan Selby. L. Newman. Mrs Brown, caretaker.

The girl did not strike him as a caretaking type. Nor did he feel she was a housewife. That left L. Newman. In flat 3.

The inside stairs were creaking like crazy as he ascended. There was an un-natural quiet which bothered him. What if she screamed when he pushed her into her room? He stifled a laugh. There had to be women like her, men on the run like him. The law of averages gave the desperate an advantage. He wouldn't wait for her to scream. He would place a hand over her mouth, whisper his intentions and see if she wanted what he could give.

He was feeling bloody randy when he reached the door with its figure 3 swinging on one nail. Maybe, if she pleased him, he would bang another nail in the number to keep it straight-up.

Placing his ear to the door, he listened. He heard softly muted music and the sound of light feet pacing back and forth. No voices.

Nothing to suggest she had a visitor. He knocked, ready to spring.

CHAPTER THREE

THOSE SUSPENSE-LADEN seconds waiting for her to open the door gave Joe the shakes. His entire life flashed across the mental screen called memory. In his skinhead days, rape had been but one of the vicarious pleasures running around with a gang allowed. During his period of employment – when he sported a Crombie and furled umbrella – getting a bird to put out for him had not always been a simple matter of dating, drinking, convincing. There had been the occasional physical taking a City "gentleman" would have baulked at.

But a man on the run had to be extra careful. Rape, as such, was great. Sometimes Joe figured the thrill of illicit intercourse more pleasurable than getting it laid on the line. The "I love you and like doing this" brigade seldom *worked* hard enough to satisfy a man. They believed in self first and if he pants for a minute he's happy.

Should he wait? Or should he skip out before it was too late?

He was debating the pro's and con's when the door vibrated and swung inwards.

"Bloody hell!"

"Yes?"

Joe wanted to grab her and do it there, in the dirty hall. His involuntary exclamation had been one of admiration. He had known many girls – and women – in his time but this one surpassed the lot. At close range he sensed her undecided desire to get acquainted, to let her passions run riot in his arms. Her sensuality seared his brain, her perfume assailed his nostrils. Yet, too, there was an inbred reserve. A with-holding that somehow contradicted her appearance.

Lottie could not compel herself to slam the door in the youth's face and lock it securely against what was so obviously burning in his eyes. In her dreams she had been confronted by many situations of a similar nature. Men shattering her door, raping her. Men refusing to be put off by her spoken denial of the emotions rampaging through her loins.

But those had been erotic dreams. This was fact. Stark, brutal fact breeding fear and indecision. Leaving her incapable of reaction.

There was, in the way they stood with the thin wedge of door offering solid – if ineffectual – proof of their "in" "out" status, something comical, and deadly serious, about the tense situation. It was as though each wanted the other to make the first, tentative overture.

Suddenly, Joe struck. His hand shot out and clamped across her mouth. His other arm snaked round her body and pushed her into the room. His heel flicked the door shut. He was breathing laboriously. Their eyes clashed – hers wide with fear, his brightly intent.

"I'll hurt you if you scream," he warned.

A low, scared moan muffled against his sweating palm.

The heat of her drove him wild. She wore nothing under the bloody dress! He could feel the velvet slide over her silken skin.

"You stood naked at the window," he accused as if seeking justification for what was about to happen.

Lottie wanted to cry. She struggled.

Joe's fingers hurt as he squeezed her face into a puckered contortion. His breathing sounded ragged, his voice harsh. "Cut that out, you teasing bitch! You're going to get screwed . . ."

She fought like a madwoman. Her knee came up, missing its target. Her hands levered between them, striving to force his body away.

"You've asked for this!" Joe released her with unexpected suddenness. As she staggered back off-balance, his fist caught her jaw. She slammed back across the room, teetered when a divan buckled her legs and fell lengthwise along it. Her dress rode high to reveal what Joe had imagined down there on the rain-swept street.

Unable to control the lust coursing vigorously through his veins, Joe quickly divested himself of damp clothing. For an instant he gazed down at the girl then, grunting, he twisted her until the velvet green dress dropped to the floor.

"I don't want her like this," he said aloud. He slapped her face and shook her. An unconscious woman would be like making love to a plastic dummy. Slowly, her eyes opened.

"Oh, God – no!" Her hand waved weakly, warding off his nakedness rearing above her.

The very sight of her moving flesh sent Joe into action. His mouth brutalised hers, his tongue probing the resisting moist cavern. His hands sought, found and fondled her lovely breasts.

She would never dream about he-men again, Lottie thought. All her varied experiences had not conditioned her for what Joe was doing. She had only known gentleness, mutually respected caresses. Not this. Not this animalistic self-gratification that left her coldly unresponsive. Even when he forced her legs apart and mounted her, she did not associate their coupling with sex. There was no heightening of sensation. None of the glorious pleasures she had found so ecstatic, so geographically wonderful in past copulations. This was like being separated from her body, like watching a man take some other woman in one of those horrible blue films her first boyfriend had insisted she watch with him.

God, how she hated this beast using her. She could have killed him and considered herself doing a public service.

Joe knew she was totally rejecting him. Not a quiver excited her flesh. She lay corpse-like, letting him piston on her coldly warm body until he could contain himself no longer. And, at the supreme moment of conquest, he sensed her revulsion.

Rolling from her he laughed. "One day you'll regret not having enjoyed me."

"You've had your fun – now, get the hell out of my flat!" Her voice sounded so unemotional, distant.

"Yeah," Joe said, roaming round the room. There was one helluva contrast between inside and the scruffy building's exterior. The girl had her place decorated tastefully. The furnishings were modern but matched the pictures, carpet and colour scheme. He particularly liked the table-lamp with its nude supporting a tassled shade. It was the first time he had ever seen a nude statue on a fixture.

"I said get out," she repeated.

Joe studied her. She had not moved since he dismounted. Her thighs were still apart, their soft inner curves slightly red where his body had frictioned against the tender skin. Her breasts had that flattened supine look so highly provocative in the object of male passion.

"You're a bloody tease," he told her. "You deliberately showed yourself at the window . . ."

She sat upright, crossed her legs and folded her arms across her breasts. "I didn't see anyone," she lied.

"Have you got a kitchen?" His other hunger had to be satisfied next.

She narrowed her eyes. This question confused her.

"Shit!" Joe stalked bare-footed into a bedroom and swore again. The girl watched him calmly now as he entered the small, compact kitchen. She had always been told her I.Q. was above average. Certain things about this youth began to make sense. She could see her evening newspaper in the magazine stand near her television set. A tremor raced down her spine. Maybe rape was the least of her worries . . .

*

"That'll keep you from trying to sneak out on me," Joe said as he tied the last knot.

Lottie frowned. The idea of spending the whole night in bed with this escaped convict did not appeal. She had no illusions regarding his ability to rape her a third time. She blamed herself for bringing on the second. If only she had kept her knowledge to herself he might have taken the few pounds she had in her purse and left during the late evening. But she hadn't. She had been so cocky, so sure that he'd run like hell.

Testing the dressing gown sash that connected his uninjured ankle to hers, Joe lay back with both elbows behind his head. It was a treat having a comfortable bed to sleep in. Since the break-out he had roughed it.

"How did you guess?" he asked.

"Rapists aren't usually starving," came her reply.

"You've had so much experience?" He laughed at his wit.

"You have, I'm sure."

Memory returned with a bang. He remembered Brighton, and how the gang had raped that bloody hippie girl. Billy had nearly let the fuzz nick him, he was so hot for the bitch.

"What happens tomorrow morning?" the girl asked.

"I'll screw you and leave."

"How can you get pleasure when I don't co-operate?"

He grinned, twisting to one side. His hand moved over her taut nipples, down the expanse of ivory silken flesh to her abdomen. He toyed with her, building her hatred into a fiery furnace. "With what you've got it's easy blowing my mind," he taunted.

"Filthy pig!"

He hit her hard. The imprint of his fingers left ugly red welts on her face. Tears sprung into her eyes and she turned her head to avoid letting him see her anguish.

"Maybe I'll beat you first," he mused to frighten her. She whimpered. This was a nightmare.

"If you made love like you meant it . . ."

She glared at him. "I couldn't – wouldn't!"

"It's your funeral," he said softly.

CHAPTER FOUR

Charlie McVey propped his morning newspaper against the ketchup bottle and poured a second cup of tea. He had expected a front page banner headline to announce the capture of Joe Hawkins for the last few days and still nothing. Not front page, not inside pages either. The little bastard was proving a slippery customer.

From the kitchen, the noise of dishes being washed intruded upon his concentration. He opened his mouth to yell, then closed it. *What the hell have I got to gripe about?* he asked himself. Not many crooks on the run have their wives keeping them company.

"Charlie, is it safe for me to go shopping?"

He glanced round and smiled generously. She looked a sight in those bloody curlers – but a wonderful sight for his prison-sore eyes. Six years makes a man wish for his wife regardless of how she looked in the early morning. Frankly, he'd taken her in preference to all those mini-skirted dolly birds the other blokes spoke about continuously in the stir.

"It's okay, Martha. They haven't circulated your picture yet."

"I'm worried, Charlie." She came into the dining room. "What if some bastard talks?"

"They wouldn't dare."

"Oh, I don't mean deliberately."

"Then what?" He was perplexed.

"That Joe Hawkins would . . ."

"Him?" McVey laughed loudly. "The little bastard doesn't know about this house."

"You're sure?"

"Sure!" He slapped her protruding rump playfully. He liked his women plump and Martha had ample flesh for what they jokingly called their cavorting.

"I'm glad you're home, Charlie." She kissed his forehead. "I wish it wasn't this way, though."

"I couldn't stay inside any longer, girl," he said seriously. "The prospect of serving another seven years porridge nearly drove me insane."

"When would you have been eligible for parole?"

"Whenever they got around to drawing my name from a hat. Is that what you wanted to hear?"

She sat heavily opposite him, face strained, eyes clouded. "I've prayed for you to quit, Charlie."

"I have – once I . . ."

Fear contorted her matronly features. Once, she had been quite a beauty but the criminal years had taken a sad toll. "He's not worth the risk, Charlie."

"He is – to me!" The man's lips formed a tight, menacing line. "Len didn't even get to see over the bloody wall."

"Len wouldn't want you to be brought back for that."

"If it hadn't been for Len's contacts I would be rotting in there." He pushed his plate away in annoyance. On his feet, he towered over the furniture. Huge hands opened and closed like a circus strongman flexing sinews before tearing a telephone directory in half. "The word is out – get Joe Hawkins and bring him to me. Afterwards," and he relaxed abruptly to smile down at his wife, "we'll be in clover street . . ."

*

Unaware that the underworld was alerted for him, Joe felt that life offered compensations for men on the dodge. In his pocket he had the proceeds of Lottie's purse and what he had managed to get for her jewellery and flat contents. Sixteen quid in all. The old pawnbroker hadn't been generous but in an area of high unemployment he had done better than anticipated.

He walked past the police station and entered a narrow side street with billboards announcing the forthcoming visit of a famous international pop group. He would have liked to stay and hear them but discretion was the stuff freedom used for crea-tive moulding.

He thought about the girl then. She would be hungry and sore before she got free. Serves her right for being such a bloody-minded bitch! If only she had made love to him the way he had sug-gested.

To blazes with her! It was no skin off his nose if she wasn't found for a week. By then he'd be in London with a few million people crowding round him as a protective shield. The fuzz would have dif-ficulty tracing him in the Big Smoke.

*

Lottie Newman found the policewoman very considerate. More so than that officious sergeant who kept trying to have his stupid questions an-swered.

"Don't worry about Sergeant Hazleton, dear," the policewoman smiled. "He's really a sweet per-son when the villains let him alone. This young Hawkins is a real swine . . ."

Lottie nodded. She hoped they would catch Joe – maybe even castrate the bastard before sending him back to prison. If ever a man deserved to be without the wherewithal to interfere with another woman, it was that rotter.

"Did he mention the names of his friends?"

Lottie frowned in concentration. She just couldn't be positive. When she had accused him of being one of those escaped convicts he had laughed and made some reference to the other mugs. But had he named people?

The policewoman tried a new tack. She understood the girl's confusion yet, too, she had a duty to perform. Not to the victims of a criminally sadistic thug but to the general public. They had to be protected from this maniac. Nothing could be done for Lottie. Not unless the girl had been mentally disturbed by the rape. Then it was for the doctors to repair the damage. Not her. Not the force.

"Did he say where he was going then?"

Lottie nodded. "London, I think."

"Did he definitely say so?"

"He spoke about his pals in the East End of London."

"Anything else, dear?"

"A lot. He was crude. He kept telling me about other women he had raped." She dropped her face in her hands.

The policewoman signalled her sergeant and placed an arm round Lottie's shoulder.

"We'd best call in the medical department," the woman said quietly.

Hazleton turned away, face flushed as anger mounted inside him.

He hated this part of his job – having to see how broken a girl could look after some pervert had had his fun. He wished to hell the politicians had not removed the birch as a deterrent . . .

CHAPTER FIVE

GEOGRAPHICALLY, Joe Hawkins was riding a lorry to nowhere. The signposts did not have any mental connections. He knew, approximately, where The Wash was, where Wales was, where Cornwall was – and there his knowledge ended. Certain place names reminded him of blokes in prison. Nobby Clarke had come from Worcester. Little Ronnie Gray from Redditch. But where the hell those towns were was beyond him. They simply existed, and that was all.

A new name flashed past as the lorry swung onto a by-pass. Cheltenham!

Christ, he hoped this bleedin' driver wasn't going there! He knew that Cheltenham had one of the most vicious Hell's Angels chapters in the entire country. Every skinhead knew that! One of the Sunday newspapers had given the bastards enough publicity to make Cheltenham a No Man's Land area for his own fraternity.

He watched for other signs now. The driver was a sullen type not given to more than grunting replies. For miles, Joe had been wondering why the man had even bothered to give him a lift. It certainly was not for conversation. That had been quickly made evident.

Cheltenham eleven miles!

The races! That was it!

Screwing round in the tight confines of the cab he glared at the horse-box construction immediately behind the small rear window. Racehorses for the Cheltenham track.

"Let me out anywhere, mate," Joe said.

The driver grunted, keeping his foot hard down on the accelerator.

"You going to Cheltenham races?"

"Yeah!" The lorry slewed round a corner and Joe gave a fleeting thought to the pathetic horses inside the box. Bloody animals getting bashed like this won't be able to run worth a damn, he thought. No wonder the bookies make a bleedin' fortune!

"Is there anywhere here I can hitch a ride to London?"

"Best chance is in Cheltenham," came the long reply.

"Is it a large town?"

For an instant the driver's eyes came off the road and brushed across Joe's tense face. "Don't you know it?"

Joe swore mentally. He remembered what he'd told the other – he had been born in these parts.

"Something funny about you, mate," the driver said then.

Joe blustered. "I've been up North for years."

"Prison, I'll bet!"

Joe tightened up inside.

The driver laughed for the first time. "I did five years on the Moor once," he confided.

The countryside had a green colouring totally alien to Joe. The small villages all seemed so neat and cut-off from the modern world that demanded a high price of its adherents. There was a tranquillity and a sense of relaxed sharing here that made Joe feel like he had entered another world. He was a stranger in paradise. A blight on this landscape. A not-belonging creature invading the peaceful haunts of a different England.

Joe shook himself and grinned as the lorry took a side-road between trimmed hedgerows. "I've been inside," he allowed.

"Thought so," the driver remarked.

"What did you do?" Joe asked.

"Manslaughter!"

Christ! A killer!

"The missus started playing around. I killed her!"

Joe wanted out of the lorry more than ever. He could visualise how the police would have this bloke's face on file, or in memory.

"Don't get the shits, kid," the driver said. Strong hands handled the heavy lorry like it was a mini. They were doing forty-five along narrow country lanes and it seemed like a ton on a motorway to Joe. "I don't like talk," the man said after some reflection. "I'm a lonely bird . . ." he laughed.

Joe got the message. Loud and clear.

"Were you in long enough to go the other way?"

He's queer! Bent! Homo! Joe inched away from the gear-stick.

"Were you?" came the insistent query.

"Naw. I like girls."

"Pity," the driver sighed and lapsed into silence.

A sign read: Winchcombe. Joe was not familiar with his history. The long, narrow street curving through ancient buildings and picturesque houses did nothing for him. It was just another community en route to Cheltenham. That this had been the county town of a Saxon region which had slowly been swallowed up in Norman re-organisation did not hit home. Nor did the ancient squabble over tobacco growing ring a bell.

"An important village this," the driver said as they made it through to the new housing estate.

"Well, it's not much now," Joe replied with disinterest. He had too much on his mind to bother about trivia. The driver's bent, Cheltenham looming closer on his hilly horizon, his need to find a large, teeming community in which to hide. These were important. Not a bleedin' county village.

"You get out or skip?" the driver asked, suddenly curious.

"Got out!"

They were climbing a hill now.

"How far to Cheltenham?" Joe asked.

"Across Cleveland Hill only."

"Where's the nearest city?"

"Gloucester – about nine miles to the west."

"Is it big?"

The lorry growled as the driver slipped into a lower gear. "Not very. Why?"

"Is Birmingham far?"

The driver laughed, geared down again. "You'd last about a minute in Brummy."

That rankled Joe. "Lissen, mate . . ."

"Go on, tell me how you beat up on old ladies," the driver teased.

Joe scowled and watched the scenery spread into a panoramic wonderland as houses and churches appeared in the valleyed distance. In the misty hinterland a range of hills started to rise, forming a sort of barrier to the view. Hotels and bed and breakfast residences formed a strip-development to the Cleeve Hill side as a few tenacious abodes clung to the steep falling-awayness on their right.

"You're on the run, aren't you?"

Joe blanched. The trouble with old lags was they knew all the signs, all the actions of that special breed of men who had spent time inside.

"Bloody trouble for me, you are," the driver moaned as they pushed in front of a bus which was about to depart its turning circle. The hill went down now . . . down, down, into the valley.

"Let me out then," Joe snarled.

"When we reach Prestbury!"

"Where's that?"

"Cheltenham racecourse."

Joe clung to his seat. The lorry careered down the incline like a run-away. Far behind, the bus formed a lessening blob against the road and the hillside. The needle was touching sixty now and Joe wanted to bale out while he was still in one piece. *The bastard wants to kill us both*, Joe thought.

Southam slipped past, a few more houses appeared and the lorry began to slow. Not fast enough. Joe knew, instinctively, that the driver was not going to make the sharp turn ahead. When a Triumph Herald swung wide as it took the L-shaped bend at speed, Joe was already opening the door . . .

*

The cab was a crumpled mess, the horses snorting furiously in the undamaged rear section. He could hear the frantic hoofs kicking hell out of the thin container walls.

People were coming and he slipped into a lane with the battered lorry forming a shield between him and the village beyond. It did not matter about the driver. He was getting what he deserved.

The stupid prick! Joe thought.

A couple of dolly-birds in mini-skirts wheeling prams came from the new estate and glanced at him. He avoided them, and hurried through the bungalow development. He liked the new constructions better than the mullioned-windowed, Cotswoldian stone facades of the older, larger residences he had caught a glimpse of before fleeing the doomed lorry. Thatched bakeries, bow-fronted windows on a chemist's shop, an old pub with ancient hanging sign and countless additions did not tempt him. He liked things modern, all glass and dull brick or, contrasting, dirt-stained and decrepit like they had in the East End.

He climbed a fence, cut across a field and came into a lane with olde worlde cottages and a main road not far away. He reached the main stem, and sighed relief. An A.A. sign with a pointing finger said: TO THE RACES. A bus ambled towards him and he spotted the stop. He ran, caught the bus and paid his fare to a small, fat, friendly-type driver. He felt strange amongst the passengers. They were too chatty, too neighbourly for his liking. None of the London frozen countenances, the dejection of living in squalid conditions existed here. Everybody seemed too happy, too pleased with life for him to comprehend their outlook.

In a way, he was glad when he reached Cheltenham's town centre. *At least*, he thought, *I'm just one of a bunch of strangers here.* Some of the types

he spotted on arrival gave him a sense of security – long-hairs, mod-geared girls, leather-jacketed
youths carrying helmets decorated with Nazi insig-
nia. His types. Ones he could communicate with
again. Not old lags, not county folk, definitely not
up-tights.

CHAPTER SIX

His types were a minority, although outstanding in a sense. The majority were well-dressed, well-fed, well-heeled. They walked with gracious airs and spoke as if carrying mouthfuls of plums between upper and lower dentures. They wore tweeds, specially-created dresses and drove away in Jags or Rolls or Mercedes. They used walking sticks, carried swagger sticks to prod aside this insectuous creature from *their* pavement.

It was Joe's first confrontation with a "county set" and he got an eye-opener. He had never known such people existed. Even his dalliance in the City where affluence and arrogance walked hand-in-hand had not prepared him for the upper-limits of Shire snobbery. What he didn't realise was that these people were friendly, sociable, if just a trifle on the borders of being too good to go to bed with themselves. Under circumstances calling for an outward display of acceptance they were as all-embracing as the local gossip in, say, Greengage or Barking Road. They had their faults but so did the great mass of people in working class areas.

I'll bet they've got some spare cash at home, he thought.

The glimmer of an idea started festering in his skull.

Catching sight of a blue uniform he sidled into a street and cut back across the main shopping centre. He had read the markers and knew now which road would take him to London. The need to get lost in East Ham or Poplar was assuming major proportions. He had to feel at home – at one with his society.

He watched a young girl leave the Co-Op store and cross the road to the bank almost directly opposite. She wasn't more than sixteen and the bag she carried suggested a snatch of some thousand or more pounds. He liked the way her ass moved inside her maxi, the way her liberated tits jiggled. *Christ, he wanted a woman again!*

A clock said 2:56. He paused, and waited. The idea was gaining impetus.

In those precious seconds prior to the bank doors closing, he counted no less than five girls of tender age entering with swag-bags visibly displayed.

What a bleedin' set-up! he thought.

Instead of hitching a ride or taking a bus to the outlying districts, he walked the streets, not conscious of distance or how his feet ached. His mind was working out the details of a super-scheme to relieve the dolly-birds of their loot. And calculating the difficulties of getting out of Cheltenham in a fast get-away car . . .

*

Plaistow hadn't altered much in his absence. Taken in small doses it stank. In large, it became a cesspool from which only the dead escaped and the living fought to eke-out a somewhat stereotyped existence. Here was an in-betweenness which was composed of gossip, wife-beating, husband-cruelty and all that small-mindedness entailed. Life, as such, in Joe's old street had always been a struggle against the intolerance of a working class fervently voting against any kind of Tory infiltration whilst wishing like hell that the Labour man had the guts to combat an ever-growing union monster.

Joe stood at the Greengage and breathed in the polluted air. It was wonderful, if rotten for his lungs. An old biddy across the street reminded him of another woman – a so-called mother whose daughter had had seven illegitimate kids before her twenty-fourth birthday.

It hardly seemed possible that less than five hours separated him from Cheltenham's completely opposite environment. The sensation of gracious living and Cotswoldian space within easy reach no longer touched him. Here there was only filth – in papers blowing along the pavements, in the grubby clothing of senior citizens, in the exterior walls of business houses.

At least, though, he felt as if he belonged here. This was his warren, his type of people.

Once he had been king of all he surveyed here. He had had a reputation, a following. Not many had dared challenge his authority in the good old days. When Joe Hawkins walked into a pub he got service with a capital S. And his word had been a law unto itself.

The need for a change of clothes, a decent meal, a place to kip and cash in his pocket, hit him hard as he watched a long-haired youth stroll from a bookie-joint counting fivers. Being on the run he couldn't ask Social Security or any of the ex-convict associations. Getting bread was up to him. But where? From whom?

In this rabbit-warren of streets and terrace houses there were guys he had known. Hymie, Billy, Don. No doubt the London press had carried the story of his fantastic escape. No doubt the local fuzz were watching his home, the hangouts frequented by his old mob. Going into any of the pubs was like asking for the beak to hand him an additional year for going over the wall. Very few of the pubs in the district were without their grass or police under-cover merchants.

What the bleedin' hell did I come back here for? he asked himself as he moved from the corner into a less conspicuous side street.

He knew the answer, as every criminal did – London's teeming millions gave more cover and more shelter than anywhere else in Britain. Nobody in the Big Smoke was a person. Each was simply a face in the crowd, a being to be ignored and pushed and thrust aside as the mass moved on its personal, selfish, all-embracing forward march.

"Christ, I've got to find somebody!" he said aloud and heard an old biddy mutter something about lay-abouts and little bleeders. He wanted to belt her, but held back. The last thing he wanted right then was to draw attention to himself.

*

Darkness was an envelope closed round him. Safe as a letter being carried by a nonentity postman he walked the streets, hands in pockets, eyes searching for just one familiar face in the boisterous throng. He noticed the increased numbers of Pakistanis occupying the pavements and found it more and more difficult to contain his urge to bash a few of the bastards. His old hatred had not been curtailed by events.

God, those were the days, for sure! he thought.

He let himself be taken and carried forward by the crowd as he recalled how the mob had followed his orders and gone on Paki-bashing sprees every so often. How they had made hippies and Hell's Angels bend a knee to their superiority. He remembered times when they had smashed a railway carriage or terrorised bus passengers on the way to a West Ham away match. Especially, he recalled the Chelsea games and those bastards at The Shed – the Chelsea skinheads!

Skinheads . . .

What was it they called themselves now? Boot Boys?

First there was skinhead.

Then came suedehead.

Now it was Boot Boys . . .

All the bleedin' same but with subtle differences creeping in to make older mobs less effective, less cemented to one leader. Many of the first brigade had married, changed their image. In their hearts they longed for the original way things had been. That he was sure of even if people denied the existence of skinheads as a force today.

The figure on the opposite side of the street looked like an apparition from some séance-directed recall-desire. He hesitated, almost losing his opportunity to shout as the shape started to enter a pub.

"Stan . . ."

The figure halted, then swung with East End curiosity and suspicion.

Dodging traffic, Joe raced across the road.

"Jesus! Joe Hawkins . . ."

"Come down here, Stan," Joe said fast.

Stan Clegge rubbed palms against his greasy overalls and darted glances up and down the street.

"For cryin' out loud – move your arse, Stan!"

Joe stood expectantly on the pavement, ready to grab the frozen youth.

"Bleedin' hell . . ." Stan murmured, moving quickly to join Joe.

"Don't say a word about my escape," Joe breathed as he drew Stan into a doorway. "Have you seen Hymie or Billy today?"

Stan shook his head vehemently. "Naw – they're both married!"

Joe felt some of the pace leave him. *Married!*

"Hey, Joe – ain't you askin' fer trouble . . . ?"

"I need bread, man," Joe replied. "How much you got?"

Stan hummed as he dug into his dirty overalls. "Not much, Joe. I'm a working slob now."

"How'd you like to split about five thousand?"

Stan stiffened and glanced out of the doorway. "Joe . . ." he wailed.

Grabbing a handful of Stan's overalls, Joe hissed: "Lissen mate – I've got a sweet set-up. We can knock off a bundle if I have the right blokes to back me!"

"The mob has broken up," Stan complained. "Anyway, I've got a job."

"Shit on that! The mob can do with some extra cash, can't they?"

Stan sheltered against a window with television sets flopping over as an example of reception in this area. He was not conscious of the programme being shown on ITV – one of those all-violent American shows which pretended to make the good guy come out on top but which never lessened the impact of crime always pays.

"How do I contact Hymie?"

Stan shuddered, then shrugged. "I'll get him, Joe! I swear – I'll get him!"

CHAPTER SEVEN

Joe Hawkins looked at the faces before him and wanted to shout a triumphant, *"I've done it!"*

Hymie, Billy, Don, Stan, Alf, Dora and Flo all stood there looking distant, aloof, totally removed from his past.

The main thing was, of course, that they had come!

That meant something!

"I've got an idea," Joe began after cold reunions.

"Forget it, Joe," Hymie snapped. "We haven't got time for your sort!"

Joe trembled.

"That goes for Dora and me," Don said with more guts than he had ever displayed during Joe's leadership.

"Let's hear it," Flo shouted, glaring at the others.

Billy shifted his feet, edging closer to Hymie and Don. His eyes refused to meet Joe's. He had grown a small beard – one of those pointed little Jewish efforts which Joe had always loathed.

"I'm against getting into anythin' bad," Billy said.

Alf Page was the oldest member of the group. He wore a Crombie, Squires and Ben Sherman. His hair was neither long nor short and his demeanour was one of total disinterest except when he asked: "Is it bread man?" and glared at Joe.

Joe winked at Alf. "Bread galore," he said.

"You're crook," Hymie said and turned, with Dora's tugging on Don's hand making it a trio of exits.

The bastard! The bitch! The weak-kneed . . .

"Forget 'em, Joe," Alf said fast.

"Look," Joe yelled, his ire up. "I'm not trying to form a mob again. I've got a certainty and I want help. It'll take four, maybe five blokes to knock off the birds . . ."

Billy shrugged and tugged at his pathetic beard. "I'm legal, Joe," he mentioned, backing to the door.

"How's about it if I tell you there's birds to screw?"

Billy hesitated, and sniffed.

"Christ, if it makes it easier for you, take my knickers down," Flo yelped.

Billy bulged hard and moved back another foot. His face was red, his eyes piggish as he glared at Flo.

"Don't you want me?" the girl asked.

"Yeah . . . yeah . . ."

Joe understood Billy's dilemma as his old mate sought for the door handle with his free hand. Billy had always liked girls – especially if he could get 'em free and willing to try something fancy. But Billy has not been the most courageous of the mob. Billy had his fear – this inborn sense of survival.

"Let him go!" Joe said as Flo opened her mouth to berate Billy when he backed out of their gathering.

Stan, Alf and Flo waited patiently as the door shut.

"Who can drive fast?" Joe asked.

Flo grinned and jabbed a finger at Alf. "He's terrific!"

"You in, Stan?"

Stan nodded and moved a few inches closer to Flo who sniffed and screwed up her nose. "You've got B.O." she said.

"I've tried everything including Lifebuoy," Stan replied with sad eyes surveying the girl's mini-skirted frame. "It's no good . . ."

"I'll say it isn't!" Flo tossed her head, then looked at Joe. "How about it?"

"I can get two blokes," Alf said.

Joe winked at Flo, then asked Alf, "Are they good?"

"The best! They've done porridge and want bread."

"Get them!" Joe went to Flo and held her against him. His hands fondled her lush buttocks. "Do you have your own pad?"

"You bet!" She brought her right arm between them and toyed with him.

"Let me know when everything's lined up," Joe said over his shoulder, too busy concentrating on Flo to bother with trivialities now.

"I'll get 'em round to Flo's tonight," Alf said as he pulled at Stan. "Come on, voyeur – we've got other work to do . . ."

*

The flat was one of those cheap, so-called furnished two rooms with kitchen effort that landlords charged the sky for in a crowded city. It required painting, decent carpets on the floor and something better than homemade tables and chairs. At half its rent it was still overpriced.

When Joe first noticed Flo she had been thirteen, flat chested and had long, thin legs. She had wanted to join his mob but he had told her to get stuffed and come back when she filled out enough.

He had no complaints now. Flo had been stuffed, and the amount of padding she had acquired in three years more than satisfied his notions of how a woman should look.

"Like?" she asked, slipping a semi-transparent nightdress over her head. She still wore brassiere and panties. Her attempts to get the briefs off gave him an adequate chance of viewing the thatching covering her loins.

"Not bad," he allowed.

"Not bad!" she wailed. "It's bloody good!" She hoisted the nightdress and left her bottom parts exposed as she deliberately unhooked her bra and displayed her pert, hard-nippled breasts.

"Not bad!" Joe said again and dropped his pants.

She eyed his nakedness and grunted. "That's terrific," she exclaimed.

"It'll fit," he said with a nonchalance she loathed.

"I take the bloody Pill," she announced as she flung herself across a creaking, sagging bed. The nightdress did little to shield vital statistics from his rampant lust.

"Just as well," he grinned, advancing on her. "They don't issue French letters in jail!" He postured above her with an obscene handling of his privates. "You don't want me to feel you up, do you?"

She touched herself and laughed. "No, Joe – I'm ready!"

He came down on top of her, positioning himself as she fumbled him into place. Their eyes met for a split-second and then he speared deep into her warmth . . .

*

"God, that was the best I've ever had," she panted and rolled off the bed. He lay like a log, gasping a little, watching her hurried sweeps with Kleenex.

The bitch in Kidderminster had been a beautiful woman; all a man could have asked for in looks and body shape. But Flo had been tops in the gymnastic department, in bringing him to that soaring height so often denied the male.

"You haven't gone without since you got out, Joe," she accused.

He grinned and held out his hand for a Kleenex.

"So what? I raped a dolly in the country."

"Cor, I like that!" She wiped him and kissed his chest. "Joe, I've always wanted to be your girl."

"Don't get your knickers in a twist," he warned. "I haven't lost the knack . . ."

"Knack?" She twisted and grabbed him, doing such sweet things he wanted to dash out for the nearest sex shop and purchase a virility tablet or six. "You've got everything it takes, Joe."

His fingers coiled in her hair and forced her to come up until her face was in close proximity to his.

"Can't you settle for just one special girl, Joe?"

He kissed her like a bull in heat, hands quickly roaming her tight buttocks, her thighs, her abdomen. As the feel of her penetrated to his emotional seat he got a mental glimpse of prison again – of randy queers trying to seduce him, of old lags saying how he was young and freshly-interesting, of cold nights doing without as the thud of a guard's feet made sleep impossible. The mood for her vanished. Pushing her away he pointed at her naked major attraction and growled: "Cover it, Flo – you won't be needin' that for a while."

"But, Joe . . ." she wailed, staring at his lean, hard body.

He dressed slowly, cogitating on the pressing problem of getting his hands on loot. Flo wasn't much even if her technique was super. What he wanted was one of those society bitch-daughters of some old Cheltenham colonel with expensive perfume clinging to her virgin flesh and a yen for it bigger than the leaning tower of Pisa. He knew the type. Had seen a few of them walking down the Promenade with their poodles and flat shoes and those cheeky bottoms wiggling like crazy. He believed all the dirty yarns told by toothy touts about the rich women who just couldn't get enough of what made them yell and swell. With bread in his kick he could call a few tunes for his brand of orgy.

By then, Flo had the message. She started dressing, sulking and darting the occasional glance at his body as he got into his clothes.

"What's been happening since I been away?" he asked.

She bent forward, let her knockers fall into her bra and jerked erect to hook the strap. "Nothing, Joe. That's the trouble."

"Don't they have an aggro?"

She pulled an old dress over her head, and palmed it down her hips and flanks. She couldn't stop trying to excite him. "Sometimes, Joe. Not like before, though. We like reggae and soul and going to discos and having a bash if some of the other kids don't fall into line, but it isn't the same. None of the old stuff."

He combed his hair, studying his face in the mirror. Time had brought its changes there, too. He was still tall – had topped the six foot mark now. His eyes, though, hadn't undergone any drastic alteration – they could blow a girl's mind if he was inclined to do so and the old coldness, the old savagery, burned in them yet. Only the prison-pallor was different – the slight greying of skin and a few extra lines round nose and mouth. That would drop away with freedom's air and being top dog again.

"Do they go to West Ham matches?"

"Every fortnight for the home games."

"What about aways?"

"Seldom." She splashed cheap scent on her dress and behind her ears. The smell of it almost made him sick.

"Can't you afford better than that?" he asked.

"Christ, Joe – I'm only a shopgirl!"

"What about your old woman?" He said it not because he was interested but for a subject to keep her talking. He didn't want to indulge in petting now. That perfume would have softened his desire in seconds.

"She's dead! Stepped in front of a lorry with the weekend shopping."

He refused to sympathise. Flo's mother had been one of his worst enemies, a woman who had called him everything.

"And the old man?"

"Stays at the Sally Ann! He went on the meth kick!"

That amused Joe. Another docker's son would find a place. He could imagine his father, Roy Hawkins, making some humane gesture like having a whip-round for Flo's old man and Ed Black shoving the collection into his pocket to cover some mythical union expense. It was a bloody mess! Dog eat dog. And, as always, the shop stewards or the union representatives came out smelling of proverbial roses while bastards like Flo's father got a flea-bag bed in a lousy Sally Ann hostel where some other no-goods were making a bomb cheating the till. What a bleedin' circle!

"You ever visit him?"

Flo burped and covered her mouth with an apologetic hand. "Not me!" she stressed. "I went once – God, what an awful place! Full of layabouts and smellin' of piss! It's a shame they get away with it!"

"God's on their side," Joe grinned and dropped the topic. He went to her handbag and opened it.

"Hey . . ."

He stared at her and she melted. Completely. He took a fiver and a oncer.

"That's all I've got, Joe," she said softly.

"You'll get a share of what we get," he replied and put the cash in his pocket.

"A boy should pay for what I let you have," she complained without making the issue a crisis.

"I should charge you for what I let you have," Joe countered and raced his comb through his hair a second time . . .

CHAPTER EIGHT

ALF LOOKED foolish when he entered Flo's flat. His eyes avoided a direct confrontation with Joe's and he stood in a servile position common to most privates being compelled to explain their failure to a stern, demanding general.

"No dice, Joe," Alf said. "The word is out – you're wanted!"

"Christ, I know that!" Joe exploded.

"Not just the fuzz . . ."

Joe tensed.

"McVey sent out orders . . ."

The memory of McVey's eyes peering at him as they made the escape came hurtling back. Joe wanted to vomit. McVey was a big man in the underworld. Bigger than a mere skinhead-cum-suedehead-cum-whatever he was now. A shiver slowly crawled down his spine and settled like an Arctic iceberg at his arse.

"Nobody wants to know, Joe!"

A prison cell, "Mad Monk" seated on a bunk cackling, with his crumpled face forming distortions against a window whose four iron bars made the sky seem as if it had been neatly partitioned, came shooting back into Joe's mind. It had been right after his second term of bird. He'd wished for a cell-mate around his own age. Instead he drew "Mad Monk" – all of fifty and as nutty as a fruitcake. But one thing he had learned from the old lag – the underworld did not end in the East End, nor in Acton, or Brighton. It reached up and down, across and beyond England's limits. It poked into Scotland, Wales, Ireland and France. It had connections and, for a price, a man could be found faster than Interpol could issue a wanted notice.

"What about you, Alf?" Joe asked.

"I dunno, Joe."

"And Stan?"

"He's chickened out!"

"Have you any connections for getting shooters?"

Alf paled. "God no!"

"Flo?"

The girl sat down heavily and crossed her legs. She had lost all enthusiasm for Joe's grandiose scheme now. "Not me, Joe!"

"Does Wilson still own that club?" Joe asked Alf.

Alf nodded with alacrity. He hated Don Wilson as much as Joe.

Trying to visualise the club brought furrows to Joe's forehead. He had only visited the place twice and then to create havoc with Wilson's mob. There was, he remembered, a rear entrance along a corridor and the front door which looked like another of the old-fashioned houses in the street. No signs. No outward display of what went on behind the "private membership" entrance.

"Wilson keeps a collection of shooters upstairs, doesn't he?"

Alf laughed bitterly. "And all loaded too! He's a mean bastard!"

"So if we got in and got upstairs . . ."

Alf brightened up and, for the first time since coming into Flo's flat, met Joe's intense gaze. "Yeah! Yeah, Joe – what we need, eh?"

Speaking more to himself than his companions, Joe paced the cramped room and gave vent to his innermost desires. "If we had guns we could really clean up a fortune. Those dolly birds wouldn't say no to handin' over the loot. And if McVey wants a showdown he can have it – face to face! Christ, this is my big chance! I've got to get Wilson's shooters! Got to!!!"

Alf and Flo exchanged worries. The girl's body had grown taut, bowed ready to send a pleading arrow at Joe's head. It was very obvious she wanted nothing to do with guns or with violence outside her ken. Alf, too, expressed his disinclination for warfare on this scale. Putting a boot in, bashing the occasional Paki or Shed fan was part of life. Not maiming somebody with a bullet.

"Are you with me?" Joe asked.

"I dunno, Joe . . ."

Flo laughed and raced hands down her thighs. "He's scared – like me, Joe. You're jumpin' the moon without a vaulting pole."

"You whore!" Joe spat. "Take her, Alf – she's randy as hell!" He strode across the room, hesitating with hand on door. "Fuck you both!" he yelled and slammed out.

*

Kenny Walker had followed trends all down the line. Very few girls had ever taken notice of him, no matter how much he spent on gear and after-shaves. He was skinny, small and had a wart on his nose which made most of his friends regard him as something just short of a freak.

He did not really belong to the East End. He had been born in Ashford but his father had been booted off the farm for paying more attention to a bottle than pigs. Now, his father worked his arse off for a peanut concern whose gimmick was stuffing bags of supposedly top-quality nuts with second rate products from Israel.

Kenny had never been sure whether or not his Kentish background or his ugliness contributed more to his castigations. He was different. That everybody knew. He spoke with a distinguishable twang and thought like a farm-boy. No matter how he dressed, he was "that yokel" ...

When Joe bumped into Kenny he felt an urge to belt the Kent youth. Then, as quickly as he had allowed the thought to enter his mind, he permitted another to invade his reason.

"Whatcher, mate ..."

For all his faults, Kenny was not the slowest thinker in West Ham. "Joe Hawkins – you're wanted!"

"So what?"

"So nuthin', Joe – I mentioned it, that's all!"

"How's every thing?"

"What do you want, Joe?"

It was Mutt and Jeff as Joe and little Kenny stood outside the television shop with its interference-blotched screens trying to entice a gullible public into buying.

"A few friends," Joe replied honestly, but deviously.

Kenny sighed and thrust his hands into his pockets. He felt the ten quid he had and promised himself that nobody – least of all Joe – was going to beg, borrow or steal his spending money.

Cars purchased on a hire-system blocked the High Street and a variety of drivers – some white, some coloured – turned as the traffic lights continued to show red. People came and stayed as the local pubs got their usual crowds. Joe remembered the days when he could walk freely into those same pubs and was treated as a special character. He thought about Mary and how Billy had made it with her. How they'd all made it with her! Gang-bang! And bleedin' good, too!

"Want to make a lot of dough?" Joe asked, sounding like an actor in a BBC *Tough Guys* movie.

Kenny fondled his ten quid and wished it could multiply ten-fold. "Yes. Joe."

"Have you got a few blokes willin' to risk the nick for a bundle?"

Kenny was interested now. He knew several youths on the outskirts of East London acceptance. Blokes like Tom Randall and Billy Bird.

"I need a driver and two hard cases," Joe said.

Tom could drive like the bloody wind! Kenny thought.

"We'll be using shooters," Joe added.

Kenny trembled. He had always thought of himself as a dab fast-draw merchant. Westerns were his favourite films. He had even spent money on one of those Canadian-made B.B. authentic six-gun models and gone down to the Old Kent Road where they made holsters to order. He figured he could twirl a Colt or draw a bead to beat the best in Britain – those jokers who frequently appeared on the telly as if they, and they alone, had the right to represent the country in an international challenge.

"Fab," Kenny chortled.

"What about the yobbos?"

Kenny frowned. He didn't like his friends being called common "yobbos".

"Sorry, Kenny . . ." Joe laughed and draped an arm round the wart-nose kid's shoulder.

"That's alright, Joe – I'll get the *blokes*!" He made sure he emphasised "blokes".

"Meet you later at—" Joe paused, trying to come up with one safe location.

"My place?" Kenny suggested.

"Great!"

Watching the small Kent youth hurry away, Joe thought – *What a bleedin' fool!* He's so grateful for being accepted he doesn't know what time of night it is!

He was whistling as he took a bus down to Aldgate and a pub where he wasn't known. A few beers, a couple of bangers and an hour listening to an old biddy chatting up an old soft bastard whose entire life revolved round beer and bed, and the idea he could still make it to the Elysian fields if only his bedmate had his king-sized (hopeful thinking) urge. After that, he knew his lot wasn't so bloody bad!

He wasn't a regular and he got the boot at closing time. Some of the others dragged and he had the impression they could stay until their cash ran out. That was Aldgate, and Upton Park, and the Elephant, and most parts of the country unless the cops had been denied privileges.

The bus back to Plaistow had a majority of Paki cutters and tailors.

He fumed, wishing to hell he had his old mob along.

He reached Greengage and hopped off. The smell of Plaistow filled his nostrils and he was not aware that, subconsciously, he relegated it to an inferior position. All he realised was that this area had been home for too many years, that here were familiarities he could touch, sense, guess about. He lit a cigarette and blew a smoke ring. *Shit on everybody living here*, he thought.

CHAPTER NINE

"THAT'S ONE," Joe said as he sat in the stolen car and watched the dolly carry her blue canvas bag across the street.

"Let's knock her off," Billy Bird said.

Joe twisted on his seat and glared at the over-anxious youth. "You stupid bastard – she's just the first! We've got to time them so we get the most at once!"

Billy shrugged and settled back against the Cortina's upholstery. At twenty one he was beyond reach of the do-gooder society's leniency. Beyond the screaming newspapers' cry for leniency. Beyond *all* leniency! A quick scan of his record would have convinced any magistrate or judge that he deserved a minimum of ten years bird. And Billy knew it!

But, he hoped – and not without reason – somebody would come to champion his "right" to go free and commit the same crime against humanity if only for a few column inches in the local, or national, press. That was the scene! The big giggle!

Tom Randall started the engine and released the handbrake. Signalling for a turn into traffic he inched the Cortina forward from the kerb.

"Where the hell are you going?" Joe asked.

Randall's head jerked once and the car smoothly slid between a lorry and a Bentley.

Joe whistled and relaxed. He had seen the copper bearing down on them at the last moment.

"If we're only marking down times we should do it on foot," Randall snarled. "I don't like to be caught with a stolen car under my arse."

Joe nodded agreement. It had been dangerously close to a *faux pas* parking on that bloody double-yellow line.

Billy started to make a two-finger gesture out the rear window at the copper who stood watching them depart. Joe's hand knife-edged across Billy's wrist. "Stupid bastard! What's the idea? Want us run-in before we make a hit?"

Billy's face showed his hatred for Joe's action. He, like the others, knew Joe's situation – that McVey had issued the word . . . *get Joe Hawkins!* It was not inconceivable that once they pulled off this job they would swipe Joe's share of the loot and make a bargain with McVey. Helping out a criminal of Charlie's standing could be more rewarding than simply settling for a few thousand. Once the fuzz caught up with him – as they would eventually for some job or another – prison could be a real home-from-home for a bloke who was known as Charlie McVey's pal.

Joe sat back and thought. Billy was worth keeping an eye on. He didn't trust the bastard nor did he believe for an instant that the youth could keep his bleedin' trap shut. But what the hell! He was already a wanted criminal and another mark against him wouldn't add too many months to his sentence. Not that he intended getting caught. He had plans. Big schemes brewing in his agile mind. The days of wine and cheese were ahead. What with Heath forcing an unwilling nation into the Common Market he could operate as easily in France as England. He enjoyed the prospect of lazing around in some Côte d'Azur hamlet with a stack of half-naked birds catering to his every sexual whim. Ambition burned strong in him. This hit would give him a start. The wherewithal so necessary to hire a gang and go for bigger and more profitable robberies.

The car entered a back street and came to a halt before a row of old houses now used as offices. He noted they were mostly real estate agents or removal firms. That fitted his mood – the desire to accumulate and become a man of property.

"Do we go back on foot?" Randall asked.

Joe considered the question. If that copper was still parading near the banks it was taking an awful chance. He grinned, letting a current thought bring him some slight amusement. "We stay – but Billy can go!"

Bird grunted, refusing to budge.

"I said you can go," Joe repeated.

"Shit on you, Joe Hawkins."

Joe's fist glanced off the other's cheek. The blow was not forceful, nor was it intended to be more than a minor chastisement. "Go!" he spat.

Billy's eyes narrowed. "That's going to be repaid in spades!"

"When you feel you're man enough," Joe smiled.

As Billy walked away from the car, Randall shook his head with evident regret. "He can be a bad enemy, Joe."

"So can I . . ."

*

Martha McVey opened the parcel and felt a wave of nausea wash over her. Her hand trembled as she gingerly removed the shooter from its oil-skin wrapper. Trust Charlie to somehow manage to have his delivered by post.

"A little beaut!" Charlie said from behind her.

"God, you take awful chances."

He grinned and patted her bottom. "Make me a cuppa. Don't concern yourself with this." He lifted the revolver and hefted it expertly. The weight told him it was loaded without opening the chamber.

"Please, Charlie – he's not worth a life sentence."

"I'm not going to kill the bastard," he said with astonishment flooding his face. "You didn't actually believe I'd stoop to murder, did you?"

She let tears roll down her cheeks. "I hope not, dear!"

He placed the gun on the table and held her tight against his bearlike hardness. "Martha, don't . . . I can't stand to see you cry."

"Forget Joe Hawkins," she pleaded.

"I can't!" He tensed suddenly. "I can't, Martha."

She brushed her tears aside. "Any news of him?"

"He made it to the East End of London but he's gone again. There's a rumble he's planning a robbery in Gloucestershire but nothing definite yet."

"Couldn't you let the coppers deal with him?"

He sighed and sat heavily in a chair. "That's not our code, and you damned know it, too! We take care of our own. He's got to answer to us for Len. The fuzz can have him afterwards . . ."

*

Kenny Walker touched his wart and scowled. Trust Joe to relegate him to keeping their B&B joint inviolate. What did it matter if the bloody prying landlady did come into their rooms? She wouldn't find anything. They had nothing to hide – yet! Not until they got their hands on all that lovely money!

Christ, how he wished he'd been given a few more inches on his frame. He realised that his weakness came as a result of lack of height. Nobody ever paid any attention to a runt. And he was a bloody runt! All his efforts at keeping up with trends were to no avail when it boiled down to conquests over girls and being somebody in a mob. He was the complete nonentity, The has-been who never had-been.

He opened a magazine and stared at frontal nudity as if the hairs could come alive and tickle his nostrils as he got . . .

He slammed the mag down on a rickety table and heard legs groan. Two pounds a night for bed and breakfast and they had the fuckin' cheek to supply beat-up old furniture! Trust the landlords. Bloody profiteering bastards!

He wanted a woman. Any woman. A nice little fresh bit from a backwoods village. A fat old cow from some farm. A hairy-lipped bitch like their landlady. Anything. He had to have something soon. He was fit to blow his mind and all . . .

*

Lottie Newman came from the doctor's office, face pale. She couldn't believe the result of her test – positive! She knew that missing one day on the Pill could have disastrous results but it just wasn't possible that she had fallen for a bastard. And that's what it would be – a bastard! Belonging to a rapist!

Why the hell didn't I accept my fate and do as that Chink said: "Relax and enjoy it!" she thought.

If only she had been more inclined to let him have his fun and butter him she could have taken her Pill on time – not after she recovered from the shock of having it savagely forced into her.

A baby – who the blazes wanted a baby?

Certainly not her!

It would ruin her figure and spoil her chances of ever finding a monied man in Kidderminster willing to undertake the responsibility of fostering a bastard resulting from her ultimate shame.

She thought hard about her torment. Pregnancy resulted not from the man's ejaculation, but a mutually responsive female orgasm. Had she actually spasmed when he reached his climax? She didn't think so but . . .

If only I could even the odds, she thought. *I'd like to see him sentenced to life!*

CHAPTER TEN

CHELTENHAM ON a Friday afternoon was a busy community. Housewives shopping for the weekend, traders busy re-stocking shelves. All the fun of the fair – and banks doing roaring business as shops sent their takings in for safekeeping.

Joe felt his shooter hard against his belly. Shoved into the waistband of his trousers, it gave him a security he had never before known. All his aggros and adventures pitted against other skinhead mobs or Hell's Angels had lacked this vital spark. Now, he was equipped to meet anybody on his terms – cordite-belching terms with death riding the explosive flame spitting from the end of a gun.

Billy Bird was down the street, loitering with intent. Kenny Walker peered into a Chelsea Girl shop for the fifth time – a poster showing nudity still the major attraction in a window display meant to appeal to girls, not blokes like a wart-nosed trendy.

Randall sat behind the wheel of a Jaguar which he had nicked the previous evening in Oxford – far enough away to give them a fighting chance of its licence number not being fully circulated here yet.

They had timed it perfectly. Five girls were soon to converge on Lloyds and Barclays . . .

Five rake-offs worth . . . how much?

Joe tensed. The girl was about sixteen, wearing a mini and flaunting her tight little ass. She stood at the kerb, hand clutching the takings as she tried to decide if there was a space she could dart through.

The other girl dodged traffic and made it to the pavement within twenty yards of Lloyds.

A third girl sauntered in the crowd and swung her blue sack containing the day's takings. She had a coat which flopped around her ankles and a pair of hot-shorts under it which revealed long legs and lovely thighs.

The woman was not being open about her chore. She hugged the paper bag close to her monstrous tits and tried to look like a housewife as she went in a direct line for Barclays.

Number five sent Joe's temperature soaring. She wore a see-through blouse and her breasts were female perfection. Her shapely thighs stood out in the crowd as she strode along in hip-shaking glory with her mini-skirt almost matching the colour of her coppery hair.

Joe moved in and saw Billy and Kenny do the same.

He was outside Barclays when the woman approached. He grabbed and got his hands on the paper bag. She screamed, stumbling back into the throng. Joe jumped forward, bag held before him. The girl in the see-through blouse stood still, eyes daring him to molest her. Joe grinned, tore the sack from her hand and hissed, "Prick teaser!" before swinging away.

Billy had cornered the sixteen year old and the second one. He slashed at the sixteen year old's face with his shooter and grabbed her takings. Blood spurted freely as she slammed hard against the wall of the bank. In less than ten seconds, Billy had the second girl cowering and had her loot.

Kenny jumped at the maxi-coated girl, seized the money, shoved his hand into her coat and gave her a feel. Her hand automatically came round and caught him across the nose with an open slap. He dropped the money and grappled with her.

Joe was already within ten feet of the car, with Billy close on his heels. Randall's head stuck out of the driver's side-window. "Kenny . . . what about Kenny?"

Joe tumbled into the car. "Get going – quick!"

Billy tore at the rear door, found it sticking and shouted: "Open this fuckin' door!"

Kenny recovered, swooped and seized the money a second time. The girl lashed out, caught him in the rounded rear and yelled.

A familiar blue uniform forced through the startled shoppers and raced towards Kenny.

The car shot into the traffic, forcing a lorry to break hard. It slewed across the road, blocking pursuit. Tom Randall grinned and sent the car into a skid for the pavement and Kenny.

The copper was only inches away from Kenny now . . .

Joe leant from the car, his shooter level.

The explosion sent the women scattering. Blood spurted from the copper's back. Kenny paled, darted round the hands-out, staggering policeman and raced for the car.

Randall gunned the engine, waited just those few split-seconds for Kenny to fall into the car and then, rubber screaming as friction burned the tyres, he shot off . . .

*

Joe counted their loot. "Five thousand quid and some change," he announced triumphantly.

Kenny sat huddled in a chair, eyes closed, hands grasped tightly in his lap. He had the shakes.

Billy got to his feet and kicked at the bed. "You cunt!" he said tightly. "You stupid cunt!"

Joe smiled and fondled his shooter which lay on the table with the money.

"Let's have my share," Randall said and held his hand out. He alone seemed unaffected by the shooting.

Joe counted out five hundred pounds and shoved it across the table. "There . . ."

"I said share – not a fee," Randall told him.

"Five hundred is good pay for driving a car."

"Not for bloody murder it isn't," Randall proclaimed.

"I killed the pig – I take the lion's share," Joe announced.

"I don't want anything," Kenny muttered as his eyes popped open.

"Give yours to Tom then," Joe laughed.

Randall took two shares, then lit a smoke. "I'll wish you life if you ever get caught, Joe," he said quietly.

Ignoring the driver, Joe turned to Billy. "Any moans in advance?"

Billy shrugged, accepted his five hundred in silence and backed across the room.

"Leave your shooter, Billy," Joe told him.

The gun came out from a side-pocket and fell to the floor with a thud.

"If you're thinking of turning me in . . ."

"Not bloody likely," Billy replied. "I'm going to inform McVey . . ."

Joe went cold.

"That grabbed your balls, eh?"

Joe's gun came up, cocked.

"You wouldn't dare blow the hideout," Billy remarked and opened the door. In a second the door slammed behind him and the sound of running feet echoed through the room.

"Another hundred for transportation," Joe told Randall.

"Three hundred," the driver smiled.

"Okay!" It didn't matter how much he made a bargain for then, Joe thought. He had no intention of paying anyway.

"In advance," Tom said.

Joe counted out three hundred. He would take it back plus Randall's two shares once they got safely out of the Cotswolds. "Let's go – London . . ."

Kenny pretended not to hear. His mind was furiously working how to extricate him from this murder charge. If he could warn the rozzers that Joe Hawkins was heading into London it might just clear him of a major sentence.

Joe walked to the door after Randall. Kenny was the least of his worries. In fact Kenny was his ace in the hole. He trusted the wart-nosed rat to blabber. He prayed Kenny would try to save his hide.

*

Road blocks on every route into London accomplished nothing. Inspector Bishop spoke to four men.

"I believe Hawkins deliberately baited a trap for us! He knew Walker would contact the police so he took a different direction."

One of the men jabbed a finger at a large-scale map on a desk. "How about Birmingham, Inspector?"

Bishop shook his head. "Not very likely. Even a Hawkins would select somewhere less probable." The inspector bent over the map, traced a road and smiled suddenly. "That could be it . . . Devon or Cornwall. At this time of year where better to seek a tourist-filled haven?"

A second man grunted. "If he's down there, sir – it could be chasing our tails!"

"We have the Jag's number, remember?"

The men nodded silently. It made sense. All they wanted was the Jaguar turning up anywhere in the country. The number had been circulated – on a priority basis. That, and that alone, would pin-point Hawkins's progress.

"We'll get full co-operation from the Devon and Cornwall lads," Bishop said. "Murder isn't their cup of tea either!"

The paper under the map gave a reason for their conference. Police Constable Norman Dawes had died in hospital as a result of a gunshot wound in the spine. A shot fired by Joe Hawkins, according to the State's witness, Kenny Walker!

*

Joe laughed as Tom Randall tried to bluff. The gun in Joe's hand made Randall's objections seem pathetically immature.

"You can't kill me," Randall said.

"I can, and will if you don't fork out the dough!"

"Look, Joe . . ."

The gun flicked and the sound of the hammer cocking filled the tranquil green with terror. Half-timbered houses slumbered into centuries' old accustomisation of violence. They had seen Roundheads and Cavaliers fighting it out on those self-same battlefields and none of the strife and mayhemious conduct had drastically changed their outlook. The green remained as a peaceful place for contemplation and cricket. The surrounding countryside stayed as it had for Doomsday recording. Only small holes in the ground and a few grave markers remained to testify to the struggles that had taken place within these precincts.

A Joe Hawkins or Tom Randall more or less would not shatter their facades . . .

"The money," Joe demanded.

Randall sighed. He was a fatalist by nature. He worked crime's fields like a farmer contending with wind and ram and bad crops. He handed over the money, conscious of the unwavering shooter pointed at his belly.

"I won't stay here, you know," Joe said.

"You'll try to make it into Wales," Randall remarked.

Joe shrugged. If that was his estimation – good luck to him.

"Do I get out now?"

"Damned right!" Joe motioned with his gun as Randall retreated to the door. Inch by reluctant inch. "You could have had the five hundred if you'd been content," Joe said as a parting shot.

"I'll have satisfaction," Randall smiled and closed the car door behind him. He stood on the green – a lonely figure lost in a country world that was not of his choosing.

Joe slipped behind the steering wheel. He was far from an expert driver. In fact, he had never held a licence. He knew just about enough to start the ignition, put the vehicle into first and steer it away.

When the car sounded like a wheezing old lady climbing Everest, he sought a new gear and rolled along with hands tight on the wheel, eyes glued to the white line separating him from oncoming traffic.

He had reached Kingswood when he decided that the effort of combatting the rush-hour was more than he dared attempt. He jerked up onto the pavement, left the Jag there and took off on foot. Public transport was much more reliable. Much safer.

CHAPTER ELEVEN

INSPECTOR BISHOP had been relegated to an inferior position. The murder of Constable Dawes called for top-level consultation and the Chief Constable had requested the Yard to assume command of the enquiry. As a professional, Bishop knew the hazards of passing the buck. A County force could, within reason, keep the Yard out. But few ever did. When a criminal roamed the length and breadth of England somebody had to guarantee a certain co-operative spirit between the various police units involved in hunting down the wanted man.

Scotland Yard had the facilities, the know-how to track clues. To keep a watch on every sector of the nation. To block ports and airfields. To get nationwide coverage of all police forces in what he considered was a strictly local investigation. He knew, now, that the Jag had been traced to the Bristol area. Knew that his finger-jabbing route had not been a pipe-dream but a spark of originality and fact. Hawkins was heading for the West Country. For Devon. Or Cornwall. To mingle with the tourists and make himself an invisible target where the chances of picking him out from the merry-making crowd was next-door to impossible.

"Are you coming to bed or not?"

Bishop stirred and gazed at his pipe. The bowl was cold. The television screen was a hum, a blankness, a sign of immersion in thought – not visual fact.

Switching the TV off. Bishop lit a match and slowly got his pipe drawing again. He could hear water running into a bath. She had plans for him . . .

He stood in the doorway of their large bathroom and eyed her nudity speculatively. She had more fat round the middle than when he last performed this ritual.

"How about washing my back?"

He grinned and set his pipe on the toilet flush cover. In a minute he had divested himself of clothes and had her soaped flannel in his hand.

"Remember how you used to do this every second night?" she asked.

"I sure do!" He rubbed down her spine, around and over her shoulder blades. He went under her armpits and onto the mature mounds of her extraordinary breasts. The nipples shot into hardness after a few swipes across them.

"Want me to stand?" she asked.

He glanced down at himself and smiled. "I'm doing that," he confessed.

She looked, sighed and huddled back to the tub's curved end. "Jump in," she said.

Unashamed, he climbed in with her, his feet sliding along the porcelain bath to grasp her flanks in their grip. His desire probed above the soaped water like a clarion call to arms.

"Want me to wash you?" she asked.

"If that's the way you feel . . ." He had reservations on what had once been considered an exciting interlude. Being a policeman, and hearing what others thought of as perversity, had softened his approach to "normal" sex. Now, he saw everything in terms of crime, sadism, perverse love-making. This so-natural arousal had lost its flavour. Its special enjoyment.

Her hands moved under the water and grasped him. Her eyes pleaded. "What about me?"

He bent forward and cursed his profession. His finger touched her hairy haven and, suddenly, he was a man again. An ordinary man. Not a policeman.

She moaned and slumped back in the water. He didn't stop what he had started. He increased the pressure, the variations . . .

Joe climbed down the ladder and viewed the beach with a critical eye. He liked some of what was there, detested the fat old ladies with their poodles and ancient husbands and settled for a stroll along the reddish sands. The cliffs rising like impossible havens should the tide sweep in gave him the willies. They were temptresses decoying shipwrecked mariners into a trap.

Nobody seeking sanctuary could scale those Devon-red crumbling slopes!

He walked through water where small creatures scattered before his advance. He heard dogs bark and saw gulls lifting on a breeze. He paid little attention to the restless sea as it foamed and churled and crested into moderate breakers forward-marching into the land. He had the isolated rock at the next cove for his target and he kept walking . . . walking . . . walking.

The girl packed her beach-bag and dusted loose sand from her lovely limbs. She had enjoyed her plunge, the battle with an incoming tide. Now, she felt the moment had come to make the trek back to safety and her hotel.

After two weeks here she understood the local problems. Along the Esplanade there were no difficulties. The shingle's rattle soon gave warning of an encroaching sea. Not so where she was. It wasn't until the water reached danger level at this particular point that one was aware of the necessity for speed. For a dash to safety where the ladder came down to link with the concrete shelf and those council-built huts.

She started down the beach and saw the youth. He seemed oblivious of the danger.

"Go back," she called and continued walking.

Joe looked at her and the bikini she sported. He visualised what was so briefly hidden and enjoyed the mental strip.

"Tide's coming in . . ."

Joe hesitated, watching a wave roll further up the beach than its predecessor. She was right. The tide was coming in. He was caught between landfalls.

"Wait for me!"

The girl kept walking, but not so quickly now.

Joe grinned, concentrating on her figure. It was something worthwhile. All motion and promises. He particularly liked the way her arse shifted inside the bikini. The way she moved from the hips. The long thighs.

He ran across the sands.

"Thanks for the warning," he panted.

"I'd do that for a dog," she said off-hand.

"I've only been here a few days . . ."

"There's a notice on the Esplanade telling about the tides," she snapped.

"I'm from London – we don't know how to read tables on tides!"

She laughed. Her pert breasts jiggled inside the bikini's scant halter. "You Londoners don't know much about anything, do you?"

Joe had a comeback, but let it slide. He wanted to ingratiate himself with this girl, and getting into a discussion on the pro's and con's of Londoners was not a way to make friends and influence a girl into his bed.

"Where are you from?" he asked.

"Warwickshire!"

He knew one town in that county. "Coventry?"

She smiled and he felt like tearing the bikini off. "Warwick, silly!"

"I'm terrible on geography," he admitted.

"So was I until I started to travel." She stepped on a pebble, yelped and hopped on one foot.

His hand touched her hip, strayed down and round and cupped her buttock as he pushed against her side. "Hurt?" he asked.

"I'm fine but isn't what you're doing being more than sympathetic?"

He squeezed a cheek and drifted his hand away as the palm slid back round the curvature of that so wonderful rump. "If it is so what? I like it!" There was a touch of the master-mistress in his tone.

"I'm not a bloody virgin but I do want respect," she snapped.

"And?" He asked the pertinent query with his eyes.

"That, too! Nothing queer, mind you."

"The normal way is fab!"

"If you're as good as the advance publicity I'm going to need encores," she quipped and leant against him.

"What's your job?" he asked suspiciously.

"I keep the accounts for a pop group." She laughed. "Pop goes some pretty teenager's knickers but never mine."

"Don't you let them know what you're after?"

"Hell, no! I'm paid to do a job – not strip every time some half-witted guitar twanger comes out of an alcoholic or pot fog. Oh, they're not bad as groups go, I suppose . . ." She drifted into thoughtful silence.

Studying her, Joe couldn't understand what made girls built for screwing come to visit a town like this one. If it had been Brighton or Southend or Weston – yes. Not this. Not where the top speed was the pace of an invalid carriage or a doddering old retired Midland's industrialist with more spare cash than sense left.

"Where are you staying?" he asked.

The girl pointed lazily to a huge hotel rising from the front. A wave lapped across her feet, a dog barked and plunged into the sea after a stick.

"Expensive?"

"I get good money," she countered.

"Can I come up to your room?"

She hesitated then burst out laughing. "You've got a bloody nerve! No, you can't. I'll meet you to-night if you wish – for a few drinks."

Joe nodded. "And after that?"

"We'll see, friend. Don't push your luck."

*

From the outside the house looked dark and dismal. Inside, it was worse. The thatched roof came down too low and the small windows in each room were almost floor level. Even in brightest sunshine there was a gloom that could not be broken.

Seated on his creaking bed, Joe thrust the girl's picture from his mind. He had four hours before he would see her in the flesh. Between now and then he had this problem . . .

Every newspaper had carried the story. The copper was dead and the hunt covered every corner of the country. An identikit picture had been flashed on the telly but the worst was coming. He knew that from this morning's editions. They had a name to go with the artist's impression now. Soon, they'd start showing real pictures of him. Police photographs.

He felt no remorse for what he'd done. Only rage for Kenny Walker. The runt had brought this about. What a bleedin' fool he'd been letting the trendy bastard in on the robbery. Jeez, how he wished that his old mob had stuck to him. They'd have pulled off the job easily – without needing shooters or getting a fuzz killed.

When he recalled some of the times they'd had, he wanted to lash out and damage furniture. Christ, he thought, what stupid idiots they'd all been! He blamed himself most for embracing a totally alien culture when he switched from skinhead to suedehead. He had played at being one. His frilly shirts, bowler, and umbrella, had all been trade marks manufactured by Terry types and necessary because he had a thing about making Mayfair his happy hunting ground.

His sojourn in prison had taught him how to look back and capitalise on previous mistakes. He was what he was and no amount of frills or environmental change could take away his East End-ness. Maybe he had lost some of his native patter, his "accent". That didn't give a damn. Inside where he lived he was Joe Hawkins, son of a docker, bigot de luxe. Aggro was his choice, his excitement. Putting the boot in on a bloody Paki or hippy or busting a Hell's Angel head stood for something terrific in his being. Being leader of a mob meant more than the loner he now was.

He counted his loot and felt the ecstasy of money flow in his veins. With this lot he could stay on the dodge and laugh at the rozzers when they were forced to admit defeat.

He didn't need an ouija board to tell him the next few days were of paramount importance. How he acted, how he stayed out of the spotlight could mean prison or freedom.

And that brought him back to the girl on the beach!

He wanted her – badly. He could taste her sweetness in his loins right then. But could he afford her? The luxury of getting her naked and thrashing under him was one he had to evaluate against years rotting away in some stinking prison.

This town was murder for the likes of him. It didn't click. It was staid and strictly for the old. He stood out like a sore thumb here. Add to this the way the local fuzz kept watching the front for deviants and he became a target for every do-gooding citizen.

Leaving his bag on the bed, he went out. There were garages and used car salesrooms nearby. All he wanted was a banger for a few hundred. Something legal to take him a hundred miles. After that, he'd flog it or steal a better model.

*

The man had an in-built slimness that manifested itself in a sneering smile and probing eyes. He bent over her like a father about to commit incest. His hand, when he asked in a silky voice what she wanted to drink, kept trying to touch her arm, her shoulder, her palm.

She waited as the man went to the bar and laughingly conversed with those residents he knew.

Damn that bloody bastard.

The image of her beach-walking "hero" turned sour. Who did he think he bloody was standing her up? She'd waited ten minutes – longer than she'd ever waited on another man. Then, she'd come into the bar and met the old geezer.

Christ, she yearned for a bit tonight – and not from her current boozing companion. He'd need splints to keep it erect! Her perfume annoyed her. What a waste of Arpège!

She fumed. She wouldn't forget that face – not in a million years! She'd remember him and if she could ever do him dirt, she would!

*

She closed the door and swore as she caught sight of her perspiration-filmed nudity in the wardrobe mirror. She flung herself on the rumpled bed and beat at the pillows with ineffectual fists.

Splints be damned! The old bastard had kept it good too bloody long. She hurt from his incessant demands. She had been pleasured alright – twice over the limit. And that made her furious.

She climbed off the bed, sniffed the aroma of sex and turned disgustedly to the television. At least that would still be working.

She was in time for the news round-up. She heard – through a self-recrimination fog – about the shooting of a policeman in Cheltenham. She saw, faintly, a picture flashed on the screen . . .

Then . . .

"That's him! That's the bloody bastard!"

She dashed to the telephone, all pain, all frustration ebbing like the sea from her heart. God, this was what she'd wanted . . .

CHAPTER TWELVE

CONSTABLE Derek Field had been a policeman since he left the army. Several times he had seriously considered quitting the force. Like when his teenage daughter had taken up with a yobbo and been involved in a brutal robbery. Not that the girl had known what was afoot. She had been a tool of a vicious thug and tricked into acting as a decoy. But the experience had shown Field how little his family saw of him and how he had fallen down on the job of fatherhood.

Another time he had tried to write his resignation had been when Marie – his wife – told him she was expecting again. At their age – then – an additional burden on his salary had seemed like the breaking straw.

But he had survived. And he was still a constable. A lonely symbol battling rising tides of vandalism and a youth revolution which decried any form of authority.

Since the beat constable had been replaced by Panda cars, Field had grown fat. And slow. Walking the streets of his small town day or night kept him fit. Seated in the heated comfort of a Zodiac had let his natural inclination to put on weight gain an upper hand. Or belly roll!

Like every policeman in Britain, Field had seen Joe Hawkins's picture. Scotland Yard had worked overtime to reproduce the mug shot and circulate it nationwide.

Armed with a list of stolen car numbers, Hawkins's picture and a description of a would-be rapist whose only claim to fame so far was three attempted "interludes" with desirable women and a warning to keep the cemetery under observation, Field drove along the road safe in the knowledge that his shift would terminate in two hours. His thoughts, even as he saw the car shoot out from a side turning without regard for on-coming traffic, were on Marie and the kids.

Tomorrow was Marie's birthday. The kids had – surprisingly – bought her a beautiful gift. His own present lay in the glove compartment – an expensive ring and matching earrings.

He goaded the Zodiac to top speed and set his lights working. He cut across the other car's bonnet and forced it into the side. He got from the Panda car and walked slowly towards the motorist. All he had in mind was a warning. A legal chastisement. He seldom, if ever, believed in booking a motorist at first sight. He thought that a police lecture gained more friends for the police and curbed more reckless driving habits than any appearance in magistrate's court.

*

Joe watched the fuzz approach. It wasn't a matter of being hauled in on a driving offence now. It was life or death. He got his shooter out and held it down by the door. He rolled the window down six inches – enough for whatever the gods demanded from this confrontation.

For a moment, Joe had the man in his sights – smack in front of the car. He held back. No driver could get a car into gear, roll forward and be sure of smashing an enemy before the target jumped safely to one side.

He waited . . .

"That was a bad mistake, sir," the policeman said.

Joe grinned. Maybe this yokel wouldn't do more than talk. He rolled the window down to its limit.

"Can I see your driving licence?"

Joe tensed. He had none. He had taken lessons in the coal lorry but had never held a valid licence in his life.

"Your licence sir!"

The fuzz peered into the car now, straining to see Joe's features in the murky disguising dark.

"I've left it at home," Joe said.

"Ahhh . . ." The policeman sounded different somehow.

"What did I do wrong?"

The policeman took a notebook from his tunic and flipped it open. A picture partially escaped and he pushed it back inside the paper. And stopped. And drew the picture out again.

Joe tensed.

"Would you step out of the car, sir?"

Joe brought his shooter up and pointed it at the fuzz.

"Joe Hawkins!" It was statement, not question.

Joe fired. He felt the gun buck in his hand, the explosion almost deafening him in the enclosed space of the car.

The policeman staggered back, hands now on his face, notebook dropping into the dirt.

Joe placed the shooter on the seat, calmly geared the car into motion and swung to avoid the Panda car angled across his lane.

*

The doctor shook his head in regret. Marie Field covered her face with splayed hands as tears rolled freely and sobs made her body heave.

"He's alive," the doctor said softly, seating himself on the couch beside the distraught woman. "Maybe, in time, he'll be able to see again . . ."

Marie cried. The small package containing Derek's present to her lay on the couch un-opened.

Across the sterile hospital waiting room her children listened to a sergeant explaining the seriousness of Derek's injuries.

Placing a hand on the woman's shoulder, the doctor felt impotent. All the advances of this modern age had not been able to cure this woman's husband. The flash and the bullet which had glanced off his temple had done their deadly work. Constable Derek Field was blind. And probably would be until he died.

"Why, doctor? Why?" Marie asked.

The doctor couldn't tell her. That was for the criminal who had done this dastardly deed . . .

*

The lights of Andover burned off to one side of the by-pass. London wasn't far away now. Basingstoke and then, *home*!

London was a trap. A gigantic underworld-infested trap. He would have to be more careful here than elsewhere in the country. But it would be worthwhile. At least he would not be an Alice lost in some lousy Wonderland full of mad hatters and crazy rabbits. He knew this warren. Knew it inside out.

His mind worked at top speed. Native cunning, the intelligentsia called it. Strictly speaking, they would anticipate him getting back to London along the M3. He detoured – across Hampshire and Surrey. Through Aldershot, Farnham, Godalming,

Guildford. He came up from the South. At Godstone, he swung into the Croydon road and dumped the car near Whyteleafe.

The sight of the gasometers gave him a wild idea which he put down quickly. It had been a lovely thought, if crazy. What a bonfire it would have made – the car covered with flames shooting upwards from those bloody tanks!

He took a bus and tried to look like an IRA man bringing a bag of bombs into London. It seemed that nobody paid those murderous bastards much heed. Christ, if only they'd turn a few thousand skinheads loose on the uppity sods the troubles would be over in a week.

The East End was out! So was Soho and central London. He took another bus and got off in Hounslow. The sound of jets roaring overhead was a comfort. He studied a few boards and settled for one ad – SINGLE ROOM TO RENT. BREAKFAST INCLUDED. There was a 'phone number but no address. He found a telephone kiosk and dialled the number . . .

*

Nancy worked every day from nine till six. Inside two minutes, Joe knew she was available. Her references to morality and the permissive society and the number of saints scattered throughout the house belied her house-coated readiness. Her eyes, too, spoke volumes.

"I'm sorry to get you out of bed at this hour," Joe said.

"Don't worry," Nancy replied and squeezed his hand. *"We understand!"*

I've got it made, Joe thought. Bed and breakfast and left-overs when the old man goes to work.

"You're not Irish," Nancy complained.

You are, bitch! Joe told himself. Her brogue could cut bacon, never mind butter.

"Isn't it awful what those Ulstermen are doing to the Catholics?"

It was an effort for Joe to control himself.

Nancy went first upstairs. She was small, dark and light on her feet. She bounced, a bundle of vivacity. "Father O'Neill says we should pray for them – and I do. Every night!" She opened a door and showed him into a sterile room with bed, dresser and a pathetically small wardrobe. "It's nice and clean," she chortled.

Joe looked at the bed. A single. He'd have a bloody job getting her worked up in such a confined space!

She closed the door. "Seven-fifty a week," she said and plucked at her housecoat so that it fell open to reveal her transparent nightdress and a cluster of hair that beckoned him like a call to arms.

He paid three weeks in advance and deliberately stared between her legs. "That should get me extra service," he said.

She was breathing hard, fast. "Mike goes to work at six every morning," she mentioned.

"I like it at night," Joe said.

She closed her eyes and swayed dramatically.

He shoved his hand between her thighs and felt her up.

"Don't be naughty," she said.

"I'm bloody randy," he told her, leaning against her.

She reached down and touched him.

"How about it?" he asked.

She groaned and pulled away. "It's a sin! It's not good for your health! In the morning – okay?"

Joe grinned. He could wait a few hours. If she couldn't relieve him then no woman could!

"Mike would kill me . . ."

"Does he sleep sound?"

She touched him again and sighed. "I can't let you . . . not the *right* way!" She squeezed him, hard. "It wouldn't waken him if I did it like this . . ."

Joe stood still as she opened his zip and started helping him attain a partial relief. Nancy had it down to pat, and upright. She knew exactly how to control his climax with her self-indulgent delight. She kept kissing his ear, moaning and moving as she handed him a pleasant interlude. Then, when it was over, she lay against him and whispered: "I'll bring you tea just after six-fifteen . . ."

"Forget the tea," Joe snapped. "Bring me this . . ." He dipped into her thighs and gave it an impromptu feel.

"Oh, God!" she moaned and tore away from him. He saw the thatch and was reminded of the place he stayed at in Devon. *Nothing gloomy about this one, though*, he thought!

Nancy backed to the door, consciously leaving her housecoat gaping, her nightdress moistly clinging to her abdomen. "Afterwards," she said with more than a little emphasis, "I'll cook a good breakfast for you!"

"Have a fast wash," Joe advised with a grin. "I don't want whatshisname getting nasty on my first night here!"

She glanced down at her hand, at her nightdress and blushed. "Oh Mary – Mother of God!" she hurled and fled.

The sexy cow! Joe thought.

He opened his bag and placed the money under his mattress.

Nancy, he felt, was a curious sort. The type of landlady who would willingly clean a bloke's room just to nose into his clothes and personal papers. She was also the right type for him at present. A stupid self-indulgent Irish bitch with a mind full of priests and Holy Water and getting what she couldn't have from her husband.

He let his mind form a picture of Mike – a big, burly construction worker or street cleaner. The type to crush a man's hand in a handshake that meant less than a trial of strength. Joe knew the Irish – knew that a firm grip in that Ould Sod meant precisely nothing. They were all a nation of heavyweight boxers a flyweight could knock over with one punch. All mouth and blarney and not much between the ears. All hatred and violence and mouth. Not a particle of generosity of feeling or sympathy for those recovering from incomprehensible terrorist tactics.

A people torn apart by religious fanaticism and a belief that the Pope would bless them regardless of what atrocity they committed. After all – Ireland was – or so the pundits claimed – the brightest jewel in the Pope's crown!

Joe undressed feeling satisfied with his introduction to Nancy and an Irish household. He had a bigger glow thinking about the morrow – and how an English "bastard" was going to contribute to the ruination of a "pure" Irish Catholic woman . . .

*

Nancy left the cuppa on a table and sat on Joe's bed. "Mister Royce . . ." That was the name Joe had given on the spur of the moment. "Mister Royce . . ." Nancy shook him a third time and heard him grunt.

She loved the shape of him outlined against the few blankets she provided. She shook him again, and saw his eyes open slowly.

"Your tea . . ."

Joe turned and lifted an arm from under the bedclothes. The hand fell across her lap.

"Wait until he leaves," Nancy whispered urgently.

Joe was fully awake now. He had been dreaming – seeing a huge Irishman tearing him apart, limb from limb, as Nancy stood by laughing and begging for more blood to splatter her carpet.

"He's in the house?" Joe asked.

"He wants to talk to you," Nancy said.

Joe accepted the tea sitting up. He wore his Chinese pyjamas he had bought from the proceeds of the robbery. The ones he liked to believe set him apart from the common herd.

"Shit!" Joe said.

"Please . . ." She didn't object to his language.

"Christ . . ."

"Don't take the Lord's name in vain," she said, conscious of her church up-bringing.

"Where is he?" Joe asked.

"Mike!" she yelled, almost deafening him.

A kindly face poked round the door within seconds and Joe was thankful he had not insisted on having a pre-tea grope.

Mike was the complete opposite of any Irishman Joe had ever seen. He stood less than five feet, looked happy and yet, if the chips were down, tough enough to take care of a man three times his size and weight.

"This is Joe Royce," Nancy said, carefully adjusting her clothing so that the parish priest himself would have difficulty proclaiming her a trollop.

"Hello, Joe. Glad you decided to take the room," Mike said and stepped inside.

Joe grinned and fell into Nancy's pattern – he pulled his bedclothes up over his Chinese pyjamas as if modesty was his forte.

"I've got to go now," Mike said and stuck out his hand. "If you like a drink there's a pub down the street which isn't bad!"

"Tonight," Joe promised.

Mike grinned and kissed Nancy on the cheek. He barely made it. She was four inches taller than him. She smiled, followed him from the room, and, as the door was left open, her voice carried back to Joe . . . "Tell Sean we'll be at the club tomorrow. I've got a present for his sister's birthday . . ."

Joe tasted the tea. It was strong, not much sugar. He jumped out of bed, opened the window and poured it out. He was back inside the sheets when Nancy returned.

"Do you want breakfast now . . . or later?" she asked.

Joe got the message and whipped the sheets back again. "Much later," he told her.

She removed her housecoat with a sly smile. "I can't be late!"

"That depends, doesn't it?"

She pulled her nightdress over her head – a different one from last night. Nude, she looked exactly what she was – a married woman with a hard body and small tits. Older than Joe wanted his women but experienced enough to give him the best possible relaxation.

"Take your P.J.s off," she said.

He shrugged out of the Chinese creations and lay naked.

"Mary, Mother of God . . ." she whispered and flung herself at him.

*

Joe reclined on the bed as Nancy used an old hanky to wipe herself. She was glistening with perspiration. And no wonder. She had given him a ride he would remember to the grave. There hadn't been anything she refused to do – and if she confessed to this lot her priest would have to devise more than Hail Marys to satisfy her continued standing in the Church community.

"Do you have any beer in the house?" Joe asked.

"Lord no! That stuff is bad for your health," she replied quickly.

"It's bloody good for my condition," he laughed and grabbed her head, forcing her to kiss his moist stomach. She moaned and tried to twist around but he thrust her away and climbed off the bed.

"Don't you want . . ."

He stared at her unashamed nakedness. "Not again." Enough was enough. The smell of sex and perspiration in the window-closed room was beginning to make him ill. Anyway, there wasn't anything he hadn't done to her, and the novelty had worn off with that last bang. She was just an older woman, a wrinkled-faced working bitch. *God yes, she is wrinkled*, he thought and hurriedly grabbed his clothes.

CHAPTER THIRTEEN

According to the *Mirror* – Joe Hawkins was in hiding in Norfolk. The *Express* believed – Joe Hawkins has been seen in Southampton. The *Sun came nearest – a bus conductor swore he had carried Joe Hawkins on his bus in the Hounslow area.

All the 'papers kept the story on their front pages. Some continued to exploit the national condemnation with editorials spotlighting youths' rebellion and this "horrible attachment to violence".

Joe read the 'papers eagerly. He had not dared watch television with Nancy and Mike. They didn't concentrate much on what the box showed and he had no intention of being in the same room with them when his picture flashed on the screen. Nancy had a habit of catching snatches of conversation or scenes and referring to people she had once known as "speaking like that" or "looking like that". The last thing Joe wanted was Nancy getting suspicious.

He had been living with Nancy and Mike for a week now. Every morning, except Sunday, Nancy had come begging for her daily ration. Twice, at night, he heard Mike banging her, too. For a keep-fit addict she certainly liked her physical jerks.

I'm bleedin' fed up with this, Joe thought as he sat on his bed and carefully folded the papers to inside pages. *I've got to get out of here!*

A train rattled past, a plane swooped low for its Heathrow landing and the entire house vibrated. Although the district was leagues above Plaistow he still hated the noise factor that threatened his sanity at times. It was like living perched on top of a volcano that growled and spat and shook so bad that every day was a suspense, a wondering when the lid would blow off.

Christ! He got to his feet and paced back and forth. The money under the mattress assumed galactic importance. What was the sense of knocking off a fuzz if he was doomed to spend his time shut up in a pathetically small room! He wanted to buy gear, to live high, to arrange another robbery with some dependable blokes for his mates.

Nancy was just another bug in his bed. Her passion for sex was driving him crazy. He had always been virile, always willing to sample illicit flesh. But this was ridiculous. The bitch could certainly shake it and move it and bring him shooting to fantastic heights. But did he want to be in the saddle with something her age? Frankly, he wanted 'em young and full of the juices of spring.

He had a map now and he spread it on the bed. Slowly, tracing roads with a ball-point pen, he considered every inch of the paper. Manchester! Now that appealed!

He took seven hundred quid and stuffed it into his hip pocket. He packed his bag and left a fiver for Nancy. The last thing he wanted was her getting annoyed at being cheated out of rent.

At seven-thirty the front door closed and he moved downstairs with his bag. They always went to the club on this night. So Nancy had said. She didn't enjoy the drinking and stuck to orange juice but she loved the group with their noise blaring through amplifiers. Mike just went for the beer apparently – and Joe fleetingly sympathised with him!

The house was empty. He dialled a number, but got no reply. It had been an impulse and he sweated blood in thanks that nobody had been at the taxi rank. God, cab drivers were the worst menace. They always remembered wanted men!

There was a used car lot not far distant. He walked and tried to console himself with visions of Manchester. He had heard it swung. And that the underworld there was just as important as London's. Anyway, it was Merseyside loosely. And didn't the United fans support skinheadism?

A long-haired youth with leather trousers and a Brando-type shirt open to his hairy navel stood on the lot. Grease covered him and his fingernails were longer – and blacker – than those old films about Fu Manchu.

Joe ignored him, picking a car strictly on price. He liked the Sovereign but they wanted too much. He almost went overboard for a sporty, low model but, again, its price soared. He settled for UVX – he nicknamed it "Uffix" for some quirky reason. It was old, a few ironed-out dents on the wings, but, generally, not in bad nick.

Grease-ball hung back as a natty dresser came up. Joe argued with him, got the car started and tried to pretend he knew a lot about engines as he feigned an ear for its running sound. The natty gent got the car out and suggested Joe take it round the block. Throwing his bag into the back, Joe hauled out his cash.

Something about the natty dresser's attitude bothered Joe. He examined the tax disc. It still had a month to run. He listened to the engine again. It did not excite him but neither did it give cause for alarm. He looked at the tyres – all with tread. Then what?

The grease-ball had vanished from the lot and Joe spotted him in the office, speaking on a tele-phone.

That was it!

Joe tore the sticker from the windscreen, count-ed out the exact money and held it out.

"I'll have to make out a receipt," the natty dresser said.

Joe held back an urge to say "forget it" and nodded. As the man hurried across the lot, Joe jumped into the car and placed his foot on the pedal. Then, he froze. If he had no receipt the bastard could call the fuzz and accuse him of stealing the car. He slammed out of the car and followed the man into the office in time to hear . . .

"Sure we're sure it's him! I tell you . . . er, yes — that's right, we buy cars, sir!"

Joe grinned. "Make it snappy, please — I've got to get to Southampton to meet a friend coming off the boats!"

Thank God for the *Express*, he thought. Greaseball seemed confused as his party squawked into the telephone. Natty dresser looked like he wanted to put an arm-lock on Joe but, instead, scribbled an official receipt. Joe seized it.

"How do I get to Southampton from here?"

Natty dresser sent a silent message to greaseball and took Joe's arm, steering him to the door. It was all so patently obvious Joe began to wonder if the world at large had formed the opinion he was a total wash-off, a nincompoop.

"Straight through Hounslow, lad," natty dresser said. "Follow the signs for Staines and the A30. You'll pick up Southampton markers."

Joe grinned. "Thanks. Hope the car makes it there and back."

He drove away, carefully following natty dressers instructions. For two miles. Then, with rubber burning, he took a series of back routes and finally reached Ealing. He wanted the M1 . . .

*

Charlie McVey raged. His wife stood naked at the sink and washed her hair, listening to his tirade with a patience she had matured over years spent hearing grandiose schemes for their future happiness and assorted plans for what Charlie was going to do to Joe Hawkins once his boys caught up with him.

"Those stupid bastards," Charlie said for the tenth time. "They let the little bleeder slip through their fingers. Why the hell couldn't they hold him? Why?"

Rinsing shampoo from her hair, the woman crossed the room and rubbed furiously with a towel for a few minutes then wrapped the damp material round her head in a turban. "Maybe they were afraid of his gun," she suggested.

Charlie nodded. "I've thought of that but bloody Ron was a paratrooper. He knows how to disarm a geezer like Hawkins!"

"He hasn't been in the army for years, Charlie!"

McVey grinned and slapped her bare bottom. "You'll get a soldier's farewell if you don't put something on."

"Chance would be fine," she quipped and flaunted her sex. Unlike most criminals, Charlie stuck to his wife. He believed in singularity in marriage. If he was desperate he gladly suffered until his arms wrapped round this one woman. He had not yet reached the stage of considering her plump, or aged. She was his missus, his choice. And when she offered he had to accept.

"You've asked for it," he laughed.

"And I hope I'm going to get it, too," she said and walked to the bedroom door . . .

CHAPTER FOURTEEN

GETTING CLOSE to Manchester, Joe began to realise that one of his prison mates had been right when he said that every county and every region of England had its own particular character and flavour. On the journey, Joe had noticed how the scenery changed, how subtle differences altered the passing villages. Now, he was very aware of the greyness, an encroaching sensation of being hemmed-in and an overall sootiness. It was as if some vital spark had been extinguished.

"Bleedin' Plaistow is bad enough," he told the fresh air blasting in from his open side-window.

He had left the motorway near Newcastle-under-Lyme. The chances of either McVey or the fuzz being able to trace his car were slim but he was determined to cut risks to an absolute minimum. He saw a new signpost: Gatley–Manchester one way, Warrington–Liverpool the other. Almost involuntarily he swung the car and headed for Warrington–Liverpool. Much as he loathed United supporters he had dreamed of being in the Kop and kicking the balls off some Scouse git. Maybe . . .

Uffix wasn't so bad. In fact, the car ran fairly well. If he worked out a deal to his advantage he could come out with fifty quid extra. That was the bleedin' trouble with being on the run. Every form of transport had to be sacrificed within set time limits. Go from point A to point B and ditch the banger! The law of the escaped. Every change of car, every new address meant an added percentage in favour of the escapee.

The shooter on the seat beside him – under a quilted jacket he had purchased for a mere three nicker – was his guarantee of reaching the next destination. Come McVey or fuzz he intended to keep rolling along!

Built-up areas filtered past his windows without reaching him emotionally. He caught sight of a poster outside a run-down newsagent's and, for the first time, began to know the meaning of fear. It said: DEMAND FOR HANGING GROWS.

Wouldn't it be just his luck if the deaths of two bleedin' coppers brought back the rope!

And he was the first to swing in ages?

The full impact of what he had done suddenly hit home! The word "murderer" seared his brain. Until that moment he had been playacting, carrying out a role destined for him even before his old man and old woman got around to tearing off a piece in a drunken stupor. Now, the value of "free choice" hit him smack in the kisser! He had not been condemned by any given rule book. All that had been part of Joe Hawkins' make-up was strictly how Joe Hawkins had wanted it. He had enveloped the skinhead cult. He had taken it upon himself to rise above his station in life and gone queer-suedehead. He alone had taken the decision to use a shooter and kill fuzz.

If only McVey wasn't against him!

*

He found a sleazy hotel near Lime Street station. His first view of Liverpool had been one of contradiction. Slums coming into the city, magnificent buildings covered in grime clinging to some century-old glory that no longer existed huddled in the partially-reconstructed centre.

Uffix was safe – temporarily. In a huge multi-story parking complex. Lost in a dark corner with two huge concrete pillars blocking snooping fuzz eyes.

For a week now he had not shaved and his beard was beginning to show signs of prospering. His upper-lip had a definite smear. Nancy had bitterly complained about these. She had objected – but only in token – when he rubbed her thighs raw with his stubble. Not that he gave a damn about the Irish bitch now. She had fulfilled her purpose. She was past tense – kaput!

Some of the dolly birds walking around Liverpool had excited him. Would they, too, complain when he got down to the essentials?

He had bought a small metal box on the journey. From a junk shop, no less. It had a key and he deposited the money in this, placed it at the bottom of his bag and layered dirty underwear across it. Next he put the bag in a wardrobe, locked this and kept the key in his pocket.

Looking from his window into a backyard filled with empty cement bags, trestles and planks, he saw Plaistow-type dilapidation all round. What looked half-way decent from the street was rotten to the brick-core out back. Supports held walls from caving in, patchwork repairs covered areas where damp and hurriedly-installed pipes had demanded urgent attention.

No wonder they're rebuilding bleedin' flats, he thought.

With thirty quid in his kick, he left the hotel, pausing in the entrance hall to glance at the telly. One of those all-knowing, all-wise bastards was holding forth about social problems and stealing a panel of experts' thunder before they could get a word in. He heard the mention of murder, policemen needing protection and the mobility of today's criminals. He smiled and stalked out of the hotel. Nothing that bleedin' idiot or his panel said would catch Joe Hawkins. Nothing they said would change circumstances. Not even public opinion . . .

*

As he came from The Wildcat Cavern with its discordant sounds shrieking at the gathering night, Walter Blair gulped air into his lungs and tried to delay his need to vomit. He felt the booze and Chinese grub swelling up into his gullet and hurried down the street to a vacant lot. He bent over a railing and spewed until he wanted to yell. The agony in his middle was something awful.

Wiping his face, Walter swung unsteadily from the railing and faced a shattering thought – he couldn't drink the way he boasted!

Admittedly, he had taken on a skinful – all day long he had been guzzling beer and shorts. The meal had been a concession to his mates. Now, he wished to blazes he had told them to get stuffed. What he blamed most, though, was that bloody place with its airlessness and the smell of pot heavy on cigarette fumes.

He hung to the railing until his eyes managed to focus. It was some change to see things as normal and not double-imaged.

"Jeez, I feel terrible!" he said aloud.

"You look worse," a voice answered.

Walter turned slowly, hand on the railing in case he got the staggers again.

"Want a beer?" the voice asked.

Walter belched. "Christ no!"

"Up the 'pool . . ."

Walter swore. "Everton, mate."

Everton? Joe stared at the swaying youth and wanted to laugh. Everton! Christ, they didn't even come into his reckoning. Maybe up here, in Scouseland, the rivalry between Liverpool and Everton was legendary but not in West Ham's fandom. Hell, hadn't Everton sold Ball to Arsenal?

"I'm for West Ham," Joe said.

"Fuckin' Hammers! Shit on them!"

Joe formed fists with his hands.

Walter belched again, swung fast and was sick for the second time. When he eventually turned he was beyond being arrogant. "Me mates made me eat Chink nosh," he said lamely.

Joe studied the other. He was lean and tallish although a few inches shorter than himself. He wore a coat with a long pointed collar, cardigan and mohair trousers with Squires. His hair was between suedehead and long and he looked like he could handle himself when sober. Or reasonably so.

"These mates of yours – are they in the market for bread?"

Walter smiled round his pallor. "You betcha."

"I've got a shooter. I'm on the run. I want a gang."

Walter felt worse. He recognised the partially-disguised features now. They'd been discussing this bastard only the other evening.

"Joe Hawkins . . ."

Walter nodded. "Yeah, mate – I know!"

"How about it?"

Walter shook his head and it hammered. "No, thanks!"

"Why not?"

"Man, who wants to get ten years?"

Joe smiled and stuck his hands in his pockets. "They've got to catch us first!"

"Like they won't?" Walter let go the railing and did a pirouette before grabbing hold again. "Jeez, I'm pissed still!" he complained.

"What's your name?" Joe asked.

"Walter. Walter Blair."

"Okay, Walter – get your mates. Let's leave the decision to them, eh?"

Walter shook his head and it hammered anew. He would have to watch that movement. It wasn't worth the anguish. "You're crazy, you know," he murmured. "Tellin' me could land you in clink."

"I'm fed up being on the run," Joe allowed. "I want mates. Guys who'll follow me. I've got plans."

"'Pool fuzz is bad," the other complained.

"We can branch out. I've got a banger . . ."

Walter felt a trifle more sober now that his gut had been cleansed. "One of 'em could grass," he warned.

"I'll take the chance," Joe said.

"It's your life . . ."

*

Walter ventured into the club and came out with five dock-type individuals. All had that "beware, I'm tough" swagger and all wore uniform – the new-look skinhead image. Their sheepskins were strictly mail order as befitted Everton fans but the rest of their gear cost plenty.

"Me mates," Walter said without enthusiasm. He still felt put on by their antics.

Joe watched them form a solid line across the pavement. He was glad he still had his shooter inside his waistband.

"Frank MacGee, Tom Carter, Doug Haskett, John Riordan and Colin Kelly," Walter said.

Bloody Irish Micks! Joe thought. *Trust me! IRA men and he was worried about them grassing! Like shit they would!*

"I've told them," Walter informed him. "I agree – we want bread, man . . ."

CHAPTER FIFTEEN

ALBERT DUCKHAM had a thing about spending half of every day at the bottom of his garden pottering around with his tomato plants and those other hard-to-cultivate items. He firmly believed that plants got to know those who tended them and could be trained to respond to loving kindness. For several years now, he had come first in the various local competitions held by the many societies catering for gardeners and allotment-holders. His marrows were, without question, the best in Lancashire. The County show had been the proof of this.

As a pensioner, Albert had no demands against his time. A day meant no more than sunshine or rain and the difference between digging and nursing and watching racing on telly. Always providing the weather was kind to him, Albert spent the day hours working diligently on his beds and peering through his trimmed edge to see how the filling station was coping with the switched-over traffic which now thundered past their village on the newly-opened stretch of motorway. It had been a surprise to find that business for the A6 had hardly dropped off.

Forking manure into a bed, Albert smiled to himself. What a stupid name for a garage! "A6" ... Now, if Brian Jones had called his station the "A6 Hopley" that would have meant something sensible.

His back ached and he placed the fork against his old lean-to with its corrugated sides. He stood erect and wheezed. His chestiness was worse today than usual. He would have to visit Dr. Knight again for more tonic.

The car entering the service area looked ordinary enough. Albert watched as young Stan Barr left his kiosk and went to the pumps. Regardless of what he personally thought about Stan's long hair, he had to admit the youngster was an excellent attendant. Nobody could ever complain about service when Stan was on duty.

As Stan inserted the nozzle into the filler, two men climbed from the car. Albert froze. He was an avid watcher of every newscast. He was also an ex-policeman. Trained for observation.

"Oh, God – no!" he moaned and rushed as fast as his creaking legs could carry him into the bungalow.

Peggy, his wife, looked up from her knitting and frowned. She didn't like to see her Albert hurry.

The doctor had warned them both – "Do anything you like but do it quietly".

"Blasted telephones," Albert growled as he jiggled the hooks.

"What's wrong?" Peggy called anxiously.

"That scamp Joe Hawkins just drove into Brian Jones's garage!"

Peggy stiffened. Something nagged at her – a dream, a premonition from the past when Albert had been walking a beat night after night.

"Hell!" Albert threw the 'phone at its mount and started to hurry towards the back door.

"Albert . . ."

The man hesitated.

"Please, dear – don't!"

The man shuffled self-consciously.

"Try the 'phone again!"

He swore, charging to the telephone. His nature demanded action yet – hell, he had promised! "Once I retire I'll never again mix in police affairs, Peggy," he had sworn.

"I'm sure Sally will answer soon . . ." his wife said, hopefully.

Albert rattled the hooks. His temper was gaining an upper hand. If only the blasted Post Office could see fit to make them automatic! They charged enough for services never given!

*

Joe smiled at Frank. John moved from the car now, too. Not another car in sight. Only this long-haired youth and a few more quid in the kitty!

Stan didn't count the crawling sensations up his spine. At first, when he accepted responsibility for evening and night shifts he had been overwhelmed by the feeling that every customer was a potential stick-up artist. He had got over this. In daylight, he was less susceptible to those old worries. Nobody would rob a service station in daylight! Nobody!

Removing the nozzle and replacing the filler cap, Stan set the pipeline back into the pump and wiped his hand on a cloth. "That'll be one-seventy-two, sir," he said.

Joe brushed his jacket aside and let Stan see the butt of his shooter. "Forget the price – let's have what's in the till."

Stan wanted to yell for help, and couldn't. It was actually happening! What he'd dreaded ever since taking the job . . .

"Move – or else!"

Stan hurried across the forecourt and into his kiosk. He placed his key in the cash register and turned it. The drawer sprang out.

"How much?" Frank asked.

Joe grinned. "Sixty-nine quid and change."

John waited until Joe moved aside and slammed Stan over the head with a tyre-iron. The long-haired youth slumped into a corner of the kiosk.

"That'll keep him quiet," John remarked icily.

Joe held the money and raced to the car. Doug was driving. "How much?" Walter asked as Joe climbed in.

"Sixty-nine plus."

"Not bad, not good. Let's get to the next one."

Frank and John took their time. They seemed to be holding back. "Get in!" Joe shouted.

"They should have more somewhere," Frank said.

"Forget it!" Joe bent forward, glaring at the pair. "Inside – we've got lots to do yet!"

John took more time than Frank. He still clutched the tyre-iron. His eyes had a wild look.

"Chicken feed," Frank said.

"Our bankroll," Joe explained, and tapped Doug on the shoulder. "Wheel it, man!"

*

Albert glared at his former sergeant. "Don't dare tell me I'm not seeing so good!" he barked.

"Al, I . . ."

"Albert," Peggy corrected.

"Albert," the sergeant said with a smiled nod to the woman. "Don't get me wrong but we all suffer from . . ."

"I saw, I telephoned and young Stan is in hospital. Does that seem like I was wrong?"

The sergeant dug into his pocket and produced a pipe. He glanced at Peggy, got a go-ahead and lit the briar. In this house he felt companionship. He had always seen fit to disagree with Albert but he would have been the first to admit that the old constable was probably the best man they ever had on a local beat. Even now, he wasn't questioning the man's eyesight. He just wanted stronger proof that Joe Hawkins had been in the car.

"How is Stan?" Peggy Duckham asked.

"Fair," the sergeant said. "He had seventeen stitches in his skull."

"Young thugs," Albert growled.

"Exactly," the sergeant agreed. "Thugs. Young. Hardly in Hawkins's class."

"He isn't old . . ."

"I didn't mean that Al . . . bert!" The sergeant grinned over his pipe and Peggy smiled her pleasure. She had always insisted that Albert was a nice name and not one to be abbreviated into the common Al. More than one copper had come a cropper trying to telephone "Al"!

"Put out an all points bulletin . . . as those American television programmes say," Albert laughed.

The sergeant shrugged. He could tell there was no shifting Albert's claim that Joe Hawkins – currently the most wanted man in the U.K. – had taken part in their filling station fracas.

"Albert's always right," Peggy said.

The sergeant took a final puff, held the pipe for it to extinguish itself and moved to the door. Albert's eyes followed him, lightly laughing.

"She knows, you know," Albert said.

The sergeant gave them both a salute – meant sincerely. "I'll be in your boat next year, Albert," he said. "And God knows, I'll need advice on how to grow tomatoes . . ."

*

The pub lacked the brass and copper of other County inns and the clientele were less inclined to accept strangers than a down-South tavern. Somehow, there was an atmosphere of severity and recognition that men only came here to indulge their alcoholic passions than to engage in conversation between a couple of half-pints.

That's another thing about the North, Joe told himself.

"What's it to be – seven pints of wallop?" Tom Carter asked.

Walter nodded fast. Frank eyed the bottles behind the bar and snapped: "Make mine Irish whiskey." John and Doug shuddered for effect and replied: "Wallop's fine!" Colin sighed. "I'd like Irish but it doesn't like me. Wallop, Tom." Joe grinned. "Same!"

Their first day as a team had been hectic but profitable. Four filling stations knocked off and a total of £280 in the kitty. All the petrol and oil had been free and they'd even managed two spare tyres for "nowt" – as Walter remarked at the time.

"Do we stay in Preston?" John asked as Tom went to the bar.

Joe thought about it. What he'd seen of the town left him convinced they were wasting their time sticking around it. All he'd been able to make out was "Fishergate" – and "Fishergate". No matter how many turns Doug made that bloody street name seemed to chase them.

"Where's the nearest swinging place?" Joe asked.

"Blackpool!" came the chorus.

Even Joe had heard about Blackpool. "That's going to be rough," he said.

"And fun," John laughed.

"I had a dolly under the pier once. From Wigan," Walter remarked. "Jeez, she bloody drained my sump!"

They laughed. It fitted with the day's raids.

"I want something bigger than filling stations," Joe told them. "How about a jeweller's store? Why not?"

"'Cause the Blackpool coppers are not going to be lenient, is why!" Frank snapped.

Tom arrived with their booze. "Grab," he shouted.

Joe belted half his down and wiped his lips. "If you're afraid . . ."

Tom stopped a quarrel. "Afraid of what? Let me in on this . . ."

Walter acted as go-between. "Joe wants to climb mountains. Filling stations are out. We hit a store next."

"So why not?" Tom asked.

"You fuckin' twit," Frank shouted. "Hittin' a shop means organisation and military precision . . ."

"And you're telling me I haven't got the ability?" Joe asked.

Frank glanced at the bulge inside Joe's pocket. "Naw, I'm against this on principle! We're doing okay – let it ride!"

"No!" Joe said. "No, I won't! I'm not content to make fifteen or thirty quid a day. I want big lolly – maybe five thousand. We hit or we split. Take your choice."

Tom said: "We hit!"

Walter finished his beer and said: "Another round and I'm for Joe."

John shrugged. "The IRA can make good use of a few hundred. That'll blow up some more Orange bastards. I'm in."

Colin grinned. "Make that double. Five hundred will buy a lot of Tommy-guns."

Doug hesitated, finishing his beer. "I'm only the driver but this could be dangerous. These fuzz have experience of setting up road blocks now. I'm not happy – I vote no!"

Frank sneered. "No for me, too!"

"That's a majority in favour," Joe declared. "If you . . ." speaking to Frank, "want out with Doug?"

"A majority drags me in," Doug said.

Frank scowled, lowered his gaze and studied a wet circle where his beer glass had been. He finished the drink, shoved the glass at Walter and said: "You got us into this – you buy! I'm in – but not willingly!"

Joe was already wondering which type of store had the most money, the most pawnable loot . . .

CHAPTER SIXTEEN

AFTER FOUR DAYS, the Blackpool "curse" permeated Joe's soul. He was bewitched, captivated, a prisoner of this Northern playground. He knew why, now, the town held such an attraction for those within a six-hour ride of its endless sands. Until this moment, Southend had been his special favourite. No longer!

From the fabulous Tower to the equally fabulous Golden Mile, Blackpool offered more deviations, more crumpet, more distractions than a thousand Southends.

Regardless of the older folk who came to relax on deckchairs and play bingo as an evening chill settled over the colourful lighting displays, Joe knew that youth could have its fling here. Promiscuous bitches paraded their wares openly. From Wigan, Bolton, Blackburn, Oldham, Preston, and all points radiating in direct lines from the "mecca" of sexual delight they came to offer unvirginal pleasures under the pier, or in shelters scattered along the many miles of secluded sands.

Secluded?

Hardly! There were more horny bastards getting to grips with willing fleshpots in Blackpool than the lecher could count. Every shelter had its private peeping Tom. Every inch of beach had its sand-dip and voyeur.

No wonder, Joe thought, *that crooks could come and go and plan big robberies here. The whole scene was open to private enterprise.*

The girl worked for a local department store. She was a cashier. She knew the procedures for collecting the cash and banking what the store considered to be over and above the safe amount to carry. She had a yen for strong, silent men with lean frames and the ability to make her coo when she wanted to coo, to make her pant when she wanted to pant, to make her. End of description!

She was a redhead – Ginger to her mates – with huge tits and a wiggle that drove her boss wild. She told Joe: "The old bastard wants to stick his hand under my shirt every time I go to the safe – and that's a laugh! He doesn't believe in being safe . . . he's a Catholic with six kids."

Joe had to admire her boss. The man wasn't so stupid if he paid attention to this choice morsel. At twenty one, Ginger had had more screws than hot meals. She admitted this. The first night Joe took her along the sands. Right in the middle of him trying to feel her up. After fish and chips at a stall along the front. Before he calculated it had cost precisely 75p for thirty five minutes of sheer bliss. Oh, she knew how alright! There wasn't anything Ginger didn't know about taking them off and finding a place under the pier and doing it so that, even from a few dark feet, it appeared that they were just petting rather heavily.

"You're terrific, Joe," she said when they had climbed to their feet. "Not gentle, mind you – but damned good when it's happening!"

"How about tomorrow night. Ginger?"

"If you want to, Joe," she said.

"I want!" He grinned, and climbed the steps to the promenade. "We could meet earlier and have a few jars, eh?"

"Great. Do you like football?"

"Yeah!"

"I can get tickets for the game this Saturday."

"Seats?" he queried. He disliked sitting down at a match. There was no fun being confined to a specific seat. No chance of putting the boot in.

"If you want the terrace?"

"That's my style."

"Won't your mates object?" She seemed to be suggesting a crowd.

"Naw – they'll go along, too!"

"Fab," she breathed and pressed a tit against his arm. "I'll wear my gear!"

*

Their boarding house was one of those tall, fifteen steps to the glass-fronted door types with carpets throughout and semi-decent furniture in every room. The landlady had not stinted on blankets, either. At the height of summer a sleeper would feel boiled under the weight of covers. The meals were satisfying considering the rock bottom prices charged. Regulations were at a minimum and the door was never locked before one o'clock in the morning.

All the houses in the street carried bed and breakfast signs, some sporting neons calling themselves exotic names like TOWER HIGH HOTEL, EL RANCHO CABANA, THE SANDS HOTEL. *A far cry from Southend's staid names*, Joe thought.

That nobody had bothered to give their place a name meant nothing in Joe's estimation. It simply had a street number, a landlady's surname and that was enough for the regulars who came back year after year to rent deckchairs and spend their holidays dashing between beach and table, bingo hall and table, boozer and late-night tea and biscuits.

Joe shared a room with Frank and Walter.

"Bloody bird wanted me to strip right there," Frank complained as he scratched his arse.

Walter smiled, and discreetly turned to remove his briefs. Joe wanted to point and cackle. He'd seen Marks and Sparks' latest creations – those multi-coloured shorts for men that had no fly and looked like a bloke had borrowed his sister's knickers. He didn't go for them. Unisex may be fine for some but he still clung to his jockey shorts with the proper outlet for manly loo-ing.

Sand fell to the carpet as Frank chucked his undershirt on his bed.

"Looks like she got you down to that," Joe remarked.

"The hell she did," Frank snarled. "She was so bloody wriggling I got more sand down my clothes than she got . . ."

Walter interrupted: "Frank, shut up! I want to hear what Joe has to say about this Ginger bit." He looked at Joe then. "Does she seem like she can be used?"

Frank spat: "Used? Christ, he banged her – didn't he?"

Joe sat on his bed. "Okay, Frank – enough! We all like nookie. That's agreed. Ginger puts out and good but she's not going to let me get information unless I butter her up. She wants us to go with her to a Blackpool game this Saturday."

"Blackpool?" the others wailed in disgust.

"They're playing Chelsea!"

"Ahh," said Frank maliciously.

"Shit!" Walter moaned.

Joe screwed his socks off and let them on the floor. "We could have some extra fun," he mentioned. "An aggro . . ."

Frank touched his ear. "With a bird along?"

"She said she'd wear her gear," Joe informed them.

"Gear?" Walter repeated and pulled his bed-clothes back. He was nude, like Frank now. All modesty had vanished in the heat of discussion. Joe had a sudden thought – *if only that randy, handy bitch Ginger was here we'd all have it.*

"She doesn't look like a skingirl," Frank remarked.

"You don't look much like a skinhead," Joe said.

"I'm bloody not," came the sharp retort. "I'm bloody Irish – and fuckin' proud of that!" Frank's jaw stuck out as if daring them to comment.

"Murderers," Joe said calmly. "Bleedin' bomb-throwing bastards!"

Frank got his hands into fists. "You're asking for it, mate," he growled.

"For Christsake," Walter groaned from under the covers. "Forget the Irish, Frank. You was born in Liverpool."

"The capital of Ireland," Joe said nastily.

"Bloody right, you London git!"

"Are we going to the match or not?" Walter shouted.

Joe glared at Frank and, for a moment, it was one of those pregnant interludes when neither party wanted to back down yet circumstances dictated the wise course was to suspend hatreds.

"Hell, I'm cutting out!"

Joe turned on Walter. "Why?"

Frank slumped onto his bed. "I'll bury the hatchet in the bastard's head after we do the job!"

Walter sighed. "Satisfied?" he asked Joe.

*

Waiting for Saturday and the match meant an extra delay in their plans. Joe was aware of mounting pressures in their camp. It was one thing to have mates and go places together for a day, or an overnight stay. It was a horse of an entirely different hue to share a room, or rooms as the case was, and expect blokes of vastly varying beliefs to get along on a friendly basis. Joe knew the root cause of their problem. They were all individualists to a large extent. They were all of a violent nature. Without exception. Some did not show this trait in speech, or in isolated deed. But, under the surface of their criminality, they exuded violence like a hot spring spewed forth a torrent of searing sprays.

Regardless of what Frank said about not being a skinhead he was the most ferocious of them all. Life, for Frank, revolved around viciousness for Protestant members of the Irish community. No outrage, no indiscriminate bombing was beyond his comprehension. Death to the Prods was his war cry. It didn't matter that some of his own people suffered the loss of a limb or eye or both. Providing one Protestant cunt got his, that justified the ends.

Irish politics left Joe cold. He enjoyed a boot-up, an aggro. He lived for a punch-up between rival factions. But he did not believe in the type of massacre Frank advocated.

Colin and John, in their quieter way, deplored Frank's outspoken desire to rid Ireland of all Protestant bastards. They had their nationalist feelings. Granted. But they did not condone the Aldershot affair or the Abercorn slaughter.

As Colin said at breakfast: "I've got Cork friends who support Manchester United. They don't want George Best murdered. If it doesn't matter in sport why the blazes should it count when women are having a meal?"

Joe, as always, jumped in. He could see Frank's simmering reply forming on his lips. "Forget Ireland. It bleedin' isn't worth fighting over – not here! For God's sake, Frank – we're out for money. Not blood!"

Frank turned a cold eye on Joe. "You should talk, *killer*!"

CHAPTER SEVENTEEN

COMMANDER Henry Hawthorne hated police work. There had been a time when he sincerely believed in the old adage that "a policeman's lot was a happy one". No longer. Since the war he had grown to loathe his job, and only stuck it out because he would collect a reasonably decent pension when he eventually retired. He could recall days when mixing with villains in his manor had been an enjoyable dalliance. Not now. The old-style villain had given way to a virulent brand of hoodlum moulded on American lines. A breed who thought nothing of using a gun, a knife, or simply booting a victim to death.

The days of chatting up a crook and knowing that sound advice was heeded, had long since evaporated into myth. The boys who carried out robberies today were beyond chatting. Beyond comprehension.

Looking across his paper-scattered desk at Sgt. Patterson, Hawthorne asked a vital question: "How do we reach this Hawkins?"

"We don't, sir," came the immediate reply.

"That seems too pat, sergeant. There has got to be a meeting point. A time and place and mental moment when it is possible to communicate."

"According to Criminal Records, sir . . ." and Patterson consulted his notebook, "this Joe Hawkins is unpredictable. He is not a common thief or criminal. He is just a kid gone wrong!"

"What the hell have we got in records these days? Bloody do-gooders? Don't hand me that nonsense about kids going wrong," Hawthorne yelled. "Kids in my day didn't go wrong. They went straight or they went bent. One or the other!"

Patterson smiled and placed his notebook in his pocket. At thirty-three he could still remember how it was to come from an area where fifty percent of the inhabitants respected the coppers and the other half tried their damnedest to get around legalities. If only to eke out a living.

"Kids in your day, Commander, didn't have to combat trends."

"You're saying skinheads and the like?"

"Those, and others," the sergeant said. "Skinheads aren't the worst of the bunch. Take the protestors, sir – the professionals like Maoists and Black Power sympathisers. They're a thousand times worse than all skinheads. Those boys play for keeps. Bombs, guns, you-name-it and they're for anything to bring this country to its knees. Anarchists, the lot! Hell, sir – begging the language, skinheads don't ask for more than an aggro and the occasional pop concert punch-up."

"And that's good?" Hawthorne asked scathingly.

"No, sir, it's not! But it isn't the worst crime. I count child molesters as the lowest of the low."

Commander Hawthorne had the decency to admit his faults. "All right, sergeant – you've won that point. Now, tell me if you want to protect Joe Hawkins?"

"No, sir – I don't."

"Why?"

"He killed a policeman – two policemen!"

Hawthorne rose from behind his desk. He had grown fat in the past few years and his belly stuck out like a seedy heavyweight's. His jowls hung and his face had a permanent flush that spoke of beer in huge quantities combined with an over-rich diet. "If skinheads aren't our prime concern why is it that the most wanted man in England today is counted as nothing more than a skinhead gone wrong?" he asked smugly.

"If we brought in a Paki and found him guilty of smuggling other Pakistanis into the country would you condemn every coloured person in the manor, sir?" Patterson countered.

Hawthorne smiled and slumped back into his chair. "I've underestimated you, sergeant. You should have been upped in rank ages ago."

"I agree, sir," the sergeant smiled coldly.

"I'll put in a notification to that effect," Hawthorne said, ignoring the sarcasm. He knew – as did Patterson – who had been directly responsible for non-promotion . . . himself! It was not too late to undo past injustices.

"Anything else, sir?"

"Yes!" Hawthorne rifled through his papers and brought out a sheet. He read it slowly, summarising for the sergeant: "Hawkins must be apprehended before he is tempted to use his gun a third time. All stops are out, sergeant. This is nationwide. We suspect he is on our manor. We'll nab him . . . right?"

Patterson shrugged. "We're stretched thin, sir. We have those two child murders and the Thornton rapes."

Hawthorne considered the current cases and reached a decision. "I've a feeling, sergeant – a hunch, if you want! Circulate Hawkins's picture to the off-duty boys for the match . . ."

Sgt. Patterson smiled. For once he inclined to agree with the commander's hunch. In seventeen years he had only known five hunches to pay off against a possible thousand. This one he liked!

*

I don't like the ground, l don't like the crowd, and I don't like the way those coppers keep staring at faces!

From the middle of the terrace, Joe Hawkins kept a watchful eye on the fuzz working round the ground. It was a difficult process to separate face from face gazing up at the packed stands, he knew. But – there was always the off-chance! That was the one he hated.

Blackpool didn't have a prayer against Chelsea. In form, the home team were capable of holding any side in the league to a draw. But their form, at present, was bad. And Chelsea were cock-a-hoop after their astonishing win over Leeds. That made the difference. Even an own goal victory had its merits.

That money Joe had not shown to his new-found friends had bought his gear – Squires, mohair trousers and colourful braces. He wore a Ben Sherman with rounded collar and a sheepskin coat. He felt right in the old groove standing beside Ginger in her check skirt down to her knees, her suede jacket with zip, her flat-heeled shoes with the crepe soles.

"You going to do a Blackpool supporter?" Ginger asked.

"Why not?" Joe grinned.

"Christ, pick a Chelsea yobbo."

"Show me one," Joe said pointedly.

"Over there . . ." She pointed and Joe tensed. It was like the old days when his mob ran rampant through every park in the league.

A long banner hung partially limp between a group with the slogan: CHELSEA FOR THE CUP just barely visible.

"What bleedin' cup?" Joe asked.

"Maybe it's for being the best targets," Ginger suggested.

Joe got the immediate impression the girl was begging for an aggro. And, if he wasn't jumping his guns, that she was more than willing to throw in her lot with a man who could satisfy her craving for violence.

"You want a boot-in?"

Ginger sighed. "God, I could be better than ever for that!"

Joe's elbow nudged Walter. "She's wet for it if we screw those Chelsea skins."

"So what's holding us back?" Walter laughed as he started to shove aside fans.

*

The kid was almost alone, shouting his foolish head off for Chelsea and Peter Osgood. He was carried away with the train journey to Blackpool and what he'd seen of the birds here. He wasn't one of the mob – he honestly believed that Chelsea were worth supporting and that the match was more important than any partisan bash-up.

A few old men stood near him, grinning as the kid yelled his lungs out every time Ossie stroked the ball or made an important contribution to the play.

Nobody bothered much about lone voices in the wilderness of Blackpool football. Middle-of-the-table would have satisfied the most hardened, most fervent 'pool supporter!

Joe got in behind the kid. Ginger to his right. Walter on his left. Somewhere behind the others followed – reluctant and filled with a no-contest detachment.

"Show me, Joe – show me," Ginger yelped.

Joe puffed out with pride. He squeezed in directly behind the kid.

"Come on – blast 'em!"

Joe tapped the kid's shoulder. "Fuck Chelsea – and you!"

The kid screwed round in his confined space.

Joe smiled, brought his leg back and planted a solid kick where it most hurt. As the kid paled and doubled, Joe smashed him in the face.

Two spectators away, another dedicated Chelsea fan saw what was happening and shouted: "Aggro!"

In seconds, the Blackpool supporters were swept aside and Joe – with Ginger squealing delightedly at his side – was fighting for his life. He wished he had a tool . . .

The shooter!

He hesitated in the middle of countering a kick and felt the boot graze his balls. He slammed a fist into the Shed boy's mouth and drew his revolver. The metal barrel slashed across another face, the muzzle rammed into a set of ivories . . .

*

Every third Saturday, Commander Hawthorne spent at home. Depending on what was showing on *Grandstand* or *World of Sport* he either stayed indoors watching telly or spent it in the seclusion of his small garden attending to the many chores which growing things demanded. He did not like seeing the nags run nor wrestlers go through sham performances to win by holds which were physically impossible or worked out in a dressing room prior to screening. He enjoyed those extra-special afternoon contests – ice-hockey from America, rugger from Down Under or a top motor-racing event broadcast live from some God-forsaken spot on the map.

This Saturday, he was in the garden. Up to his wrists in fertilizer. Sweating from turning over soil for yet another bed of his wife's favourite flowers.

The telephone jangled a discordant noise on the tranquil air. His wife came from the sunporch. It was for him . . .

"Hawthorne," he said when he finally took the receiver.

"Hawkins has been positively identified as being at the match," Patterson's voice told him.

Hawthorne felt a wave of satisfaction wash over him. "And?" he asked.

"Afraid he got away, sir – there was an awful eruption in the crowd!"

Hawthorne swore – loud and long. He had another hunch – that lapse could cost them all!

CHAPTER EIGHTEEN

GINGER ROLLED onto her back and opened her thighs. She was naked, her clothes lying on the sand near them. Joe had his clothes round his knees, poised above her.

"Yes, Joe, yes . . ."

He withheld his pleasure.

"God, don't make me wait!"

Joe came an inch closer, and felt her respond to the temporary touch of flesh on flesh.

"What do you want from me?" she wailed, struggling to join them together.

Joe whispered, keeping his buttocks arched to prevent her from gaining the final gratification. He kept whispering and making hurried explanations until she was writhing with demented frustration.

"Yes, Joe, yes – I'll do it! Just go into me . . ."

He slammed hard against her, hearing the whoosh of air from her lungs as she seized him in passion-steel legs. She was beyond anything but the most basic four-letter talk. She surged and gave, straining to match her companion's violence of that afternoon. She had been eagerly wanting this moment ever since she saw her hero in action. Now, the accumulated desires burst forth and devoured him . . .

*

"He's an old nanny," Ginger said as she pulled her skirt back on. "I could convince him to let the loot build up if I thought it was worth my effort!"

Joe stopped her in the middle of a wriggle. His fingers moved over her abdomen. "For me?"

"God, yes . . ." She yielded to his grope.

"What's the best day?"

Ginger moaned and flung herself supine on the sand. "Night, Joe . . . night!"

He stopped fondling her. "Pull yourself together," he ordered.

"Christ, you're terrific!"

"The best day?" he reminded.

"Monday's hopeless," she panted. "Usually the weekend. Friday morning or Saturday late afternoon."

"How much on a Tuesday?"

"A few thousand . . ."

"That's all?"

"Well . . ." She squirmed and grabbed hold of him again. "Joe, please?"

"After this . . ." He stuck his hand up her clothes. He knew she was loving it and trying hard to concentrate on what was most essential to him. "Well, what?"

"He carries a float of about two thousand but that's always locked in the safe . . ."

"You could make him open it, eh?" He fingered her.

"Christ – that's beautiful!" She wormed closer to him. "Yes. I could . . . Oh, Joe – I'm ready!"

He stopped asking questions and concentrated on bringing her those joys she found most exciting. It wasn't hard to provide her with additional thrills – she was jelly waiting to be devoured . . .

CHAPTER NINETEEN

Doug had insisted on having a different car for their escape. According to him, Uffix had guts but no stamina. In a chase stamina was vital. Against police-mechanic tested vehicles, the criterion was an ability to keep going at top speed for an unlimited number of miles.

Uffix failed in a relatively simple test. Along a stretch of the M6 between Garstang and Lancaster, it failed to keep up with, or pass, a Hillman. That, in Doug's book, left it wanting.

Armed with his unblotted licence, Uffix for trade in and another hundred quid of Joe's money, Doug went searching the car lots for a bargain capable of holding police cars at bay.

"Do you know the side roads?" Joe asked.

"I should!" Doug sat like a martyr and munched on his roll with cheese. "When you bastards have been busy screwing I've been driving round every back alley in Blackpool! I can get out of this town in ten minutes – and that doesn't count police blocks, either!"

Joe smiled. "You deserve an extra one percent."

Frank scowled. "Why? He's only driving the car!"

"Can you get us out?" Joe asked.

"No – but . . ."

"You fuckin' Irish bastard!" Joe exploded. "All mouth and nothing between the ears!"

"I'll take an equal share if all goes according to plan," Doug said hurriedly.

"That's up to the Mick," Tom Carter said.

Colin stepped in with a broad Paddy smile and a lot of Liverpudlian common-sense to boot. "He's not a Mick! He's Dublin-Protestant of all things! But shit on that – we're not fighting Ireland's war. We're fighting for a prize worth a few thousand . . . and I, for one, would like a slice of that!"

Joe stood facing his "mates". "Is everybody agreed?"

"I'm for Ireland but meself first," John Riordan laughed.

"Money, not bloody politics," Doug snarled.

"Same here," Walter agreed.

Tom Carter stepped forward and glared at Frank. "You bastard! You no good bastard! The trouble with you is you're scared to make a real stand! You're always shootin' off your mouth but what have you ever done? Nothing. That's what. You're so scared of being clobbered you hide behind anybody – even Shiela! For once, meet it like a man – say yes or no and don't shit me with what fuckin' Ireland needs or hasn't got!"

"It hasn't got anything," said Colin softly.

Frank eyed his companions, meeting nothing but hostile stares. He twitched, knuckled his fingers in his lap and dropped his gaze . . .

"So?" Colin asked firmly.

"I didn't hide behind Shiela," Frank finally said.

"No?" Colin shot upright and stood within inches of Frank. "How come she cried her bloody eyes out to me when you left the United game without getting an aggro?"

"I didn't meet up with a bloody United supporter."

"The hell you didn't!" Colin paced back and forth between the beds in the room. "You were smack in the middle of the cunts!"

"Who says . . ."

"Shiela!"

Frank melted slightly. "She was mistaken! I heard a few of 'em shouting but . . ."

"You didn't have a bomber or a bunch of the bhoys, eh?" Joe chortled.

Frank dissolved into pathetic nothingness.

"I'll give you five quid and that's all," Joe said. "As from now . . . fuck off!"

Frank looked at his mates.

"He's right," Walter said. Colin, Doug, Tom and John nodded.

"You'll be sorry," Frank muttered.

"I wouldn't grass," Joe said.

"I certainly wouldn't," Colin agreed.

Frank directed his venom at Joe. "We'll meet again, one day!"

"If we do – don't bother to say hello," Joe retorted.

Frank silently got his belongings together – including the fiver Joe threw on the bed. When he had packed he went to the door.

"If you grass you'll be worse off than an IRA squealer," Joe said.

Frank tossed his head in the air and left . . .

CHAPTER TWENTY

In the North, Blackpool's reputation stood for many things but, chiefly, for its ability to cater for every member of a family without fear or favour. Elsewhere, the image of Blackpool conjured up dreams of dolly birds putting it out on sand or shelter, and con men out-shouting each other in an effort to entice the unwary into gimmicky exhibits.

Television had not treated Blackpool with kid gloves. Those who had, at some time or another, considered the Golden Mile as an expanse of shimmering sand and little else had been rudely awakened from the dream state by the portrayal of a fairground come-on artist as nothing less than a trickster.

Another programme had shown the Northland's playground as a haven for randy rugger players and mill girls willing to go into a tackle together.

Factually, Blackpool was a little of both with a generous helping of middle-aged deckchairism for a catalyst. Unlike Margate, Southend and Brighton in the South-East, Blackpool's popularity with the near-retired had not been dented by hooliganism. There was room enough for all – miles of glorious sand, a pleasure beach capable of supporting any teenage invasion, and a town that continued to grow annually. Probably what saved the resort from becoming a ghost town was the availability of a copper. At the height of the troublemaking season, it seemed there was a blue uniform every few hundred yards – a solid figure keeping out of the mainstream yet there, ready to pounce and prevent disturbances reaching gigantic proportions.

Joe was far from happy by the number of fuzz dotted round the town. As they drove slowly down streets he got the impression that every corner was a hangout for one of the officious bastards. He counted fifteen coppers before they reached the department store.

"Is it always like this?" he asked Walter.

The Liverpudlian shook his head in wonderment. "I don't know! I've never seen this many!"

"I wonder if that bloody Frank . . ." Doug started to say.

"He wouldn't dare," Colin snapped.

Joe was not quite so sure. Frank had struck him as a vindictive person. If Frank had grassed . . . He felt panic but brushed it aside when Doug parked near the store.

"I'll go in first. When Ginger sees me she'll get the manager worked up!"

Colin laughed. "That bitch could make a brass monkey get hot balls!"

Joe smiled. It was a matter of pride. Ginger had not even glanced at his mates with anything but the barest of interest. She belonged to him. And the others were bleedin' jealous!

"What happens to her?" John asked.

"She goes with me!" Joe sat back and waited for the anticipated yells. He had arranged this with Ginger – after all, she was a good screw and she could finger them all if she was left high and dry. Unknown to his mates, Joe's future plans did not include them after today. Once Doug had them safely out of Lancaster, Joe and Ginger were splitting.

"I thought you'd tell us that," John said softly.

"I'm not in favour but I'm not going against it, either," Walter said.

Doug grinned. "She'll be our ace in the hole. The fuzz wouldn't dare try anything dangerous with a girl in the car!"

Joe waited as Colin digested the words. He could see that Tom was playing a waiting game, too. Wanting the last say.

"If we're all in this together then Ginger belongs to us, right?"

Tom chuckled. "Randy bastard!"

Colin nodded. "She's some piece."

"That's your price?" Joe asked quietly, trying hard to stop his hand closing on the shooter.

"My only price?" Colin said.

"All right. She's communal property," Joe announced.

The others stared at him. Joe felt mighty important. He had proven beyond any shadow of doubt that he could handle situations without displaying his innermost feelings. If words could integrate them then words would get the show on the road. What he said and what he meant did not correspond. Mentally, he swore and wanted to kick each of them where it hurt most. And he would – after they pulled off the job! After they cleared the police network!

Tom got out of the car and stood on the pavement. "Come on, let's collect our bang!" he said with a guffaw.

*

Ginger spotted Joe immediately he entered. She suppressed a tremble and gave her full attention to a couple she was serving. She felt no surge of adrenalin. Only emotion. Joe's brand of loving had captivated her. No other man had ever made her react so hysterically, so irrationally.

When the couple departed, Ginger closed her till, removed the cash and went straight to the manager's office.

This was the difficult part. Her vamp role had to be spontaneous and she hoped to convince the man that she had finally fallen for his furtive handling of forbidden fruit. It would be a supreme test of her womanly wiles. One she had thought about all the steepness night.

It wasn't even as if she had time to perfect her act. Joe had been adamant. Ten minutes flat – no more, no less.

In her estimation, Horace Black was a mother's boy with a demanding wife. As a man, he rated less than half a star in her book. His six kids did not count, either. They were the result of a church demand for more converts and a fruitful mate.

Her flesh crawled as she entered the office with its disorganised sheets littering two desks, till rolls scattered across a third and glorious piles of money already banded for the bank . . . Joe's bank! . . . on Black's safe.

"Why, Ginger – what are you doing here?"

The girl smiled – weakly. "I don't feel so good. Mister Black. I thought you wouldn't mind if I had a break!"

Black simpered, his eyes automatically racing over her lush figure. The girl always set him off. There was that sensual something about her that started his hormones working at disastrous top speed. She reminded him of the woman he should have married. The woman his mother had accused of being a non-Catholic slut.

At forty seven he should have known better than to become enamoured with one of his shop girls. He knew the risks attached to liaisons of this kind. He also realised that his occasional uncontrolled handling of Ginger's person left him wide-open to a criminal charge. Yet, he didn't care. She was an obsession. A desperate need!

"Sit down. Ginger!" He jumped to his feet, hurried round the cluttered desks and placed his hands on her sides. The touch of her was excitement. Heady stuff. He helped her into a chair, hands trailing upwards to lightly brush against her swelling breasts.

"Mister Black!" Ginger expressed surprise – and a coy liking for what had happened.

Something snapped. This was the first time she had ever permitted him an encouragement. Previously, she had flushed and stormed out of the office . . .

"Ginger . . . oh. Ginger . . ." His hands cupped her marvellous breasts and he bent forward, his lips planting kisses on her throat.

Christ, he's as stiff as a poker! Ginger thought as she watched him progress to madness.

He was struggling with her bra through her clothes, guttural sounds coming from his chest.

"Oh, God!" Ginger moaned, touching him.

He went crazy. He got on his knees, pushed her clothes up, began kissing her soft warm thighs as his hands probed higher . . . higher.

Bloody bastard! The filthy swine!

Ginger pushed his head away, his hands, too! She forced herself to look composed – if a trifle emotionally disturbed. "Not now. Mister Black . . . let's be sensible. Put my takings in the safe . . ." Her eyes darted at the locked box.

"Yes, Ginger . . . yes!" He stood, not at all embarrassed by the thrusting evidence of his lust.

Her watch said nine minutes since she had entered the office. She got off her chair, let him feel her nearness as he fumbled with the combination lock. "Hurry, Mister Black – I'm all . . ." She leant against his shoulder, breathing heavily in his ear. "I'm all wet . . ."

His fingers were thumbs but he managed to flip open the safe. Perspiration rolled down his face. It was an effort to refrain from raping her.

"Give it to me," he panted.

He was completely unaware of the office door opening, of Joe Hawkins coming across the room.

"You're a darling, Mister Black," Ginger whispered and quickly jumped aside.

Joe's shooter descended and crunched on Black's skull. The manager slumped, hand clawing down the safe door as he faded into unconsciousness.

Joe laughed, a brittle echo for the departed. "How much?" he asked as Ginger started to empty the safe.

"About four thousand – we had a good morning . . ."

*

Doug geared down for a sharp bend, and sent the car screaming into a series of twists as the road wound through a built-up area with school-crossings and crossroads galore.

"Four thousand, eight hundred and forty nine quid," Joe counted from the back seat.

"Bloody hell!" Colin exploded.

"Oh, Joe . . ." Ginger inched closer and kissed Joe's cheek. He could feel her increased warmth – a result of what she had undergone and the natural reaction to having this much wealth within reach.

From the front of the car, Tom's laughter sounded hysterical. "Jeez, ain't it sweet!"

Walter in the back looked glum. "Let's divvy, Joe."

"Now?"

"Bloody right! Ginger's hot . . ." said John, and Colin echoed this with: "That's no lie!"

"Fuck you bastards!" Walter snapped. "I'm not thinking of a screw."

"Sorry – go ahead," Colin graciously consented.

Ginger giggled and placed her hand on Joe's upper thigh. Any reference to her "ability" gave the girl a thrill.

"Joe," Walter continued with a finger indicating Ginger's non-mercenary interest. "I'm not against birds having a right share in the spoils but when they can only think of sex then I'm scared stiff!

She's crazy for it, man. And that could be trouble. I want out. Now! With my cash!"

Joe had to admit that Walter's tirade was a saving grace. If only he could convince the others of the necessity of baling out then all his problems were solved at a stroke. Like Ted Heath, he had opportunity on his side but unlike the Prime Minister, he had freedom of action to settle his disputes single-handedly. He didn't have powerful unions resisting his decrees. He didn't have class warfare to contend with. He had mates – erstwhile, admittedly – and Ginger . . . a real redheaded angel in disguise.

"Okay," Joe said. "I'll split the haul. We all agree to split, eh?"

Doug sent the car into a tight turn and straightened out with difficulty. "Knock the cost of this off my share and I'll be content."

Joe counted the money into equal amounts. There was a little over. He pushed that to Ginger. "Spending money for clothes," he said and handed each their divvy.

Walter looked foolish as he accepted his share of the money. "Sorry, Joe, but . . ." He stared at Doug. "Let me out at the next bus-stop!"

Tom and John sighed, placing their wads in their pockets. "Me too," said John. "And me," said Tom.

Colin eyed Ginger speculatively and shrugged. "Shit!" he said. "I'll get out as well!"

"How about you Doug?" Joe asked.

"Did I cop the car?"

"Yeah – but I want to be driven to a place where I can get another," Joe said.

"How about Accrington?"

"They used to have a football team," Joe laughed. "That's okay with me . . ."

*

Ginger sat with skirt pulled up around her knickers and chewed gum. Every so often she reached across the seat and stroked Joe's arm. She was not aware of the countryside flashing past the windows. She only had her thoughts and the scent of her man not far distant from her.

"Is London really swinging?"

Joe kept the speedometer needle holding the eighty mark. Nothing had managed to pass them for the last fifty miles. He enjoyed the thrill of speeding by lumbering lorries and cautious legal-speed-limit passenger cars. He was a bloke in a hurry. A bloke with somewhere to go, something to do.

"The greatest. Ginger," he said and placed his hand on her sleek thigh. The world was treating him like a prince. He had this, and lolly. Nothing could stop him now. Not the fuzz, not McVey. He had all the bastards beaten. He would keep them on the hop. Joe Hawkins was smarter than all their specialists and all their underworld informants. God, how he loved the almighty feeling permeating his being!

CHAPTER TWENTY-ONE

FOR FIFTEEN YEARS, David Newbery had been in and out of prison with a regularity that astounded probation officers ordered to present evidence in court. Regardless of his convictions, David had somehow wangled the minimum sentence for each charge brought against him. That he was a plausible bastard did not lessen the astonishment of those who interviewed him. Even the beaks sometimes expressed wonderment at their own leniency when confronted with his record in the privacy of their chambers.

Of course, David had one thing going for him. He was a nark. He could no more go straight than a corkscrew could extract a cork without its twists. But he had a reputation for supplying the fuzz with information leading to arrests and convictions they could not normally have achieved. For that, and that alone, he got treated with a certain degree of leniency!

He had just pulled off a successful robbery but his trademarks pointed conclusively to him. In an effort to gain sympathy, he grassed . . .

"I was conned into it, sir," he told Detective-Sergeant Knowles. "There was this bleeder called Hawkins . . ."

Knowles felt a tremor of satisfaction race down his spine. Hardly a copper in Britain dared hope that a nark would come up with such a juicy piece of data.

""'E forced me to open the bleedin' safe, sir!" Newbery added.

A wave of triumph passed through Knowles's frame. "Did he say where he was staying?"

Newbery paused, sweating blood. "Do I get orf?"

"That depends, David."

"The bleeder's important, eh?"

"We want him – yes!"

"Drop the charges?"

"Not entirely – but we'll make them no more than three months!"

"Christ!" Newbery exploded. "That's bleedin' robbery!"

"Suspended?"

Newbery laughed. "Six months?"

"Agreed!"

"And you let me have two days freedom?"

Knowles considered the request. "Okay – where do we find Hawkins?"

"I've got to check, guv'nor!" David said.

"Two days and the high jump if you don't come up with Hawkins," Knowles said.

"I'll find the bleeder," Newbery stressed . . .

Playing both ends against the middle was nothing new to David Newbery, and being accused of double-dealing did not deter him from his life of crime. As a "peterman" he was unique. There wasn't a safe he couldn't crack in less time than a fuzz had a coffee at the canteen. He had an affinity for mechanical trickery where safes were concerned. No matter how many precautions the manufacturers put into their products, David had the answer in advance. He knew, instinctively, that changes had been made and how to circumvent them.

The underworld, in general, knew that David grassed to protect himself. That was why so many of the people behind David's capers refused to identify themselves. Masks and various other methods of camouflage were always the *modus operandi*.

Except in the case of Joe Hawkins!

Joe wasn't a member of the clan. He had heard how good David was with a peter and he farmed-out the job accordingly. It was another Ginger getting the boss hot for her! Another soft touch!

*

Way back before pot and pornography on the newsstands, the club had catered for a clientele verging on the elite – writers, television personalities and showbiz generally. No more. Since the very young took over Soho and made the scene one of youthful enterprise, the club's management had sold out and the customers had dwindled until, now, only those searching for near-virginal applicants for perversion sessions bothered to come.

People like Newbery were accepted because they could be used. People like Joe and Ginger because they were young and notorious. The youth rebellion liked their martyrs!

"S'truth, mate – it's a dyed-in-the-wool cert!"

Joe listened with half-an-ear. He was only conscious of Ginger pressing her sizzling loins against a randy bastard with fuzzy, long hair and tight jeans which showed where he was heading.

"Christ, Joe – ain't you interested?"

Joe got to his feet, face tense. He shoved through the gyrating crowd, and stood in front of Ginger and her partner. "Back to the bench," he told Ginger.

The fuzzy-wuzzy glared at him, and deliberately rubbed himself on Ginger.

Joe growled and tore the girl from her dancing partner. "You bleedin' asked for this, mate," he snarled and lashed out with his foot. He felt the blow jar his thigh. Felt satisfaction travel along his leg.

The fuzzy-wuzzy doubled, clutching his groin.

Nobody stopped to pass comment. Nobody bothered.

"Back to your seat," Joe commanded.

Ginger walked back to where Newbery sat in a state of near-paralysis.

"You was saying?" Joe asked as he sat opposite the peterman.

"Jeez . . ."

Joe grinned. "That's only friendly stuff. Imagine what he'd got if he'd double-crossed me!"

David Newbery suddenly reached a conclusion. This was outside his league. He was an amateur playing in a strange, unfathomable combination featuring unrealistic creatures. His type had gone by the boards of progress. The old-style professional creed no longer counted. The new was uppermost, and unless he got to recognise the changes he could easily be the late David Newbery!

"The coppers asked me to finger you," David blurted.

Joe smiled, content with this advance information.

"They suggested the set-up!"

Joe felt Ginger's thigh. "And?" he asked.

"They want you, mate! Want you bad!"

"How bad?"

"Enough to let me get off with the last job!" This, to Newbery, was tantamount to a carte blanche approval of all his activities.

"We'll do it," Joe announced.

"Fuck me!" David said.

"And me," echoed Ginger . . .

CHAPTER TWENTY-TWO

Inspector Bishop and Commander Hawthorne got the news simultaneously. Each man wished he, personally, was on the squad keeping watch as Joe Hawkins pulled yet another job. Neither of them had much confidence in the Metropolitan officers handling the "arrest". They had adequate proof of Hawkin's durability, his ability to evade traps.

Outside the warehousing area, Joseph English, distributors to the magazine trade and owners of a string of shops dealing in near-pornography, fifteen officers attached to South London division waited.

From information received via Newbery channels, the hit was tonight. Not tomorrow as originally scheduled.

It was a cold night. The warehouse looked like a huge concrete block standing against the moon in white angularity. It was windowless except for one small four-squared section above the printing plant. And this did not warrant observation.

Not in police eyes . . .

Above the single opening, Joe dangled on a rope held by David and Ginger. He had rigged a pulley but it still required the expertise of two companions.

"Down . . ." he called softly.

The rope stretched and he jerked down . . . down . . .

"Hold it!"

He fumbled with the loose catch, using a celluloid strip supplied by David. The catch opened. He levered it upwards, held it against the ratchet and called: "Next!"

He was almost totally inside the building when David descended the rope.

Joe smiled to himself. The bleedin' fuzz would be wild when they discovered that their grass had betrayed them for gold . . .

Sergeant O'Malley watched Joe Hawkins climb down the rope into the warehouse area. All the reports he had received showed Hawkins as a bad lad! Especially as he was also wanted by Charlie McVey. O'Malley had his own sources of information. Most of them were strictly contrary to Home Office edicts. It was enough, though, that O'Malley and his parish priest hated the current goings-on in Northern Ireland and had formed a pact to filter information regarding this religious campaign down through channels.

A priest in Liverpool had passed along data. A priest in Birmingham had passed it further. O'Malley had the full data . . .

O'Malley waited patiently. He was directly beneath Joe as the "bhoy" reached six feet above the concrete floor of the warehouse.

There was no going back! No possibility of reaching for the shooter that had brought about two deaths already.

O'Malley held his arms out – huge Irish arms with a power of restraint in their embrace . . .

"Don't struggle bhoyo," O'Malley said.

The accent brought a lump into Joe's throat. Of all the bloody people to arrest him . . .

THE END

SKINHEAD

(OPENING CHAPTERS)

CHAPTER ONE

Outside the shed, a freighter blasted the lunch-hour silence with her whistle. The churn-churn of props frothed the Thames as a Liberian registered vessel slipped from her berth, holds battened down on the vital exports bound for South Africa.

Inside the shed, surrounded by an untidy clutter of unloaded merchandise, the dockers relaxed – sandwiches eaten, tea brewed and being sipped, the flick-flip of cards the only sound they wanted to hear.

Jack Boyle grinned across the upturned crate at his mate Roy. "Whatcha doin', Roy?"

Roy Hawkins studied his cards for the fourth time. He wasn't much of a poker player. Solo was more his game. "Blowed if I know, Jack."

Ed Black leant across Roy's shoulder and snorted disgustedly. "Pack 'er in, Roy," he offered. "Let me take your seat an' I'll show you 'ow the game should be played!"

Roy glanced at Jack and got a nodded agreement in return. Slowly, he replaced his coins inside his dirty overalls, carefully stacked his hand on the discard pile and relinquished his seat. He didn't mind. He had only taken a hand because Ed had to see a union representative at the gates. "What happened about the meeting?" Roy asked as Ed slumped into his place.

Ed set twenty quid on the table with a flourish. He fancied himself as *the* poker player of all time. His claim to fame was his ten hour visit to Las Vegas when sailing the P. & O. line to Vancouver and Japan. He never let his mates forget how he managed to sit in on a game with Red Skelton and come out showing a profit of six hundred dollars. What he forgot to mention was his subsequent call at a Gardena, California club and the loss of that six hundred plus every British penny he had in his pocket.

"Jack's got 'em by the short and curlies," he said loudly. "They got until Monday to meet our demands..."

"And then?" Roy asked, stuffing tobacco into his old briar.

Jack gathered the cards and started to shuffle the pack. His attention was focused on Ed but it didn't stop him doing an expert job and dealing five cards to each member of the school.

"Then we go out," Ed announced.

Roy scowled. He didn't like strikes. He believed in Jack Dash; believed in a working man's right to withdraw his labour for better pay. He didn't believe in frivolous disruptions of work – and, in his opinion, this latest episode was decidedly petty. "I'm against it Ed," he said.

Black spread his cards tight against his chest. He was a canny man; a distrusting individual. He studied the cards pointedly then, having proved his superiority, glanced leeringly at Roy. "You'll do exactly as Jack says!"

Roy nodded. *Yes*, he thought, *I'll follow the bloody band. I dare not go against it.* He believed that Jack Dash was the man closest to God; believed fervently in the right of the docker – and every working man – to take measures to combat the capitalistic employer. He was completely disenchanted with this Labour government – but he wouldn't abstain nor vote Tory. He would vote Labour as he always had; as his dad and his granddad had. It didn't matter what he said between elections – that the long period of Tory rule had been the best in living memory – providing that when the day came, he could make his "X" against the local Labour party candidate. In his constituency, Plaistow, the ineffectual hands on the helm of England counted for less than a man's worth to an employer. 1926 and the "cloth-cap" image had to be preserved. Forgotten were the affluent days of Tory rule. Forgotten were the massive debts piled on a staggering nation by yet another Labour administration. It didn't count that Britain was being dictated to by the International Monetary Fund.

"Are we playin' cards or discussin' the political situation?" Jack Boyle asked.

Ed Black glanced at his fellow-docker.

Roy smiled, puffing contentedly on his briar.

Solly Goldbluff smacked a fist into his palm and demanded, "Fuck the politicians and Jack Dash. I've got a hand – when are we goin' to play cards?"

Ed glared at Solly now, relinquished his platform to the determination showing on that Jewish face. He had never understood Solly; just as he had failed to appreciate Roy's hostility to the Labour movement as specified by extreme adherents like Dash. He knew that Roy would follow along in the main-stream of opinion; knew that Labour had an unswerving vote from Hawkins; knew too that the disenchantment Roy felt was common to the majority of trade unionists. Yet, he was assured by "cell" leaders, Roy and his mates would vote as usual when the crunch came.

Studying his cards, Ed shouted, "I'll open..."

Roy watched the game with lessened interest. He saw his mate win the pot; saw four other hefty hands go to Jack. Then, suddenly, it was time to return to work.

"It's a bleedin' shame," Jack Boyle said as they stepped outside the shed, "that Ed has it in for you, mate."

Hawkins shrugged and puffed on his pipe. "Oh, he isn't so bad."

"Like hell! He's a rotten bastard..." Jack's antagonism boiled over as Ed stepped from the shed with four of his special cronies trailing behind like bodyguards, ready to prevent physical harm to their adored leader. "Why don't you let Joe do him?"

Roy ignored Jack's suggestion. It was enough that he claimed fathership to the lad. He didn't have to be reminded what a rotten little bastard his son was nor to inflict him on one such as Ed Black. Basically, Roy was decent; law-abiding within the limits set by dockland. He did not consider pilfering a crime; it was a docker's perks to purloin Scotch and foodstuffs and the occasional costly items from "broken" packing cases. In the old days, Christmas would have been a barren table if it hadn't been for the goods stolen from the docks. Mostly, the employers and the police turned a blind-eye to the petty stealing. Only the capitalistic insurance concerns made a hue and cry about the extent of dockland thievery. Like so many of his mates, Roy didn't stop to consider that £10 a month taken from somebody else's pocket could multiply into a fantastic sum when set against the total number of dockers in the nation.

"'Owabout it, Roy?" Jack insisted.

"Forget Joe," Roy growled. "I have..." He tapped the tobacco from his pipe and prepared to mount the gangway of a Norwegian freighter.

Boyle frowned. He couldn't understand Roy's attitude toward his own son. In his opinion, Joe Hawkins was only doing what all of them should do – have a go at authority. Jack was a rebel out and out. Only his hatred for Ed Black saved him from being classified as a militant – plus, of course, his friendship for Roy. He needed somebody like Hawkins to temper his viciousness; his addiction to causing trouble.

An hour later, Jack found himself forced to work with Ed. In a far corner of the hold, Roy slaved with a dedication Jack found sickening.

"Christ, doesn't 'e know when to stop?"

Ed Black welcomed the opportunity to take a break. He wasn't a man who enjoyed hard labour nor did he consider it necessary to kill oneself for the employing body. His creed was simple – "higher pay for less work." Productivity agreements were, to him, a means to an end. They sounded fine on an engineering contract but, in reality, they meant absolute zero in action. His brother in the *Mirror* had kept him informed of *their* productivity agreements and it was a family laugh when they discussed the way that union had buffaloed the government's prices and incomes policy.

"'E's a blackleg, Jack. I don't trust 'im."

Boyle moved away, wishing to hell he hadn't opened the door for another Black tirade. Roy and he may not always agree, see eye-to-eye, but they were mates. Which was more than could be said for Ed Black. Ed was nobody's mate. "I wouldn't annoy Roy unless you want to meet up with his son, Joe."

Ed jabbed a finger into Jack's chest. "That little bastard isn't interested in the likes o' me. 'E ain't even worried about 'is old man."

"It isn't wot Roy said," Jack threw back, hopefully. "I wouldn't annoy Joe Hawkins. Not ever!" He shook his head thoughtfully.

Ed Black was thoughtful too. He was big, strong, had taken care of himself in some weird corners of the globe. As the union representative, he could count on certain heavies to protect him during a strike. His cronies would always rally round his particular flag, too. Yet – the mention of Joe Hawkins sent a shiver of fear down his spine. He couldn't understand this modern generation. Violence was a natural part of life as a docker saw it but the style of brutality these kids employed frightened him silly. Fists and the occasional kick happened; clubs with nails sticking through, and boots specifically meant for inflicting serious injury, were something else again. It wasn't just Joe Hawkins that worried him. One yellow-spined kid would never worry the likes of him. But Joe had a mob and even he was forced to admit that one man was no match for a bunch of savage little bastards ready to tear an individual apart just for fun.

"I'll talk to Roy," Ed said softly, moving away from Boyle.

Jack grinned. Slumping against grain sacks, he waited for Ed to return. When the union specified it took two men to lift what an old-time docker would have considered an easy weight, Jack believed in obeying rules. Two men it would be; and every lost minute meant a fatter pay-packet anyway!

Joe Hawkins hated his parents with all the violence in his young body. Especially, he loathed his father's attitude to life. What, he asked himself as he washed meticulously, had his dad gained from being a soft touch? The house they lived in was far removed from a palace. It was small, cramped, in an awful street. The neighbours were old, foul-mouthed and unintelligent. Not that Joe felt that he possessed a good measure of intelligence. He admitted, but only to himself, that his education had suffered badly. But he was foxy clever. He had a native intelligence that would carry him to heights his father had not inspired to reach. Plaistow and its dirt were not for Joe. One day, he would move away and never return. His sights were set on a plush flat somewhere near the West End. But that required money, and social position. And, as yet, he had neither, although his day was coming. Of that he was positive…

"Joe… you upstairs?"

He turned from his wardrobe mirror and scowled at the partially open door. His mother sounded in a vile temper – as usual!

"Yeah."

"Come down 'ere."

His hand automatically reached inside his shirt for the comforting feel of the tool stuck in his trousers' waistband. He was proud of it. He had taken a week to make the weapon – thick rubber tubing filled with lead-shot and sand, and plugged securely until it was pliable without losing the necessary sting when used. Dropping his shirt over the cosh he slowly descended the narrow stairs.

"I arsked you to fetch me bread this mornin'," his mother snarled. She waved a loaf before his face, "'and over the money… this is stale!"

Joe grinned. "It was all they had."

"The money!" Mrs. Hawkins said again, hand outstretched. Joe didn't frighten her. She was one of those heavy women with massive forearms and a determination to match her girth. She had been born in Plaistow and fought for everything she had.

All her life, Thelma Hawkins had known poverty and hardship. Unlike her husband Roy, Thelma did not have cause to trust her neighbours nor believe in anything except herself. Even her son was an object of suspicion where it came to money.

"I ain't got it," Joe sulked.

Thelma's heavy hand swung, catching the lad across his cheek. "Joe," and she breathed heavily, "I'm not arskin' a second time."

The boy's hand dipped into his pocket and handed over a coin. Thelma sighed, fingered the coin as a priest would a statue of the infant Jesus. "Next time I arsk you..."

"I won't bleedin' go!"

Returning to his room, Joe contemplated his face in the mirror. Her hand-marks showed red. "The old cow" he muttered, fondling his cosh, wishing to hell he could get enough courage to use it on her. Pleasant dreams flooded his mind – and, he saw his hand streaking down, the cosh a blur as it slashed across her cheek, the sound of cracking a satisfactory end to a fleeting wish.

He fingered his face momentarily, then swung from the mirror with an exclamation of frustration.

Opening the wardrobe, he selected his gear from its shadowy recesses...

Union shirt – collarless and identical to thousands of others worn by his kind throughout the country; army trousers and braces; and boots! The boots were the most important item. Without his boots, he was part of the common-herd – like his dad, a working man devoid of identity. Joe was proud of *his* boots. Most of his mates wore new boots bought for a high price in a High Street shop. But not Joe's. His were genuine army-disposal boots; thick-soled, studded, heavy to wear and heavy to feel if slammed against a rib.

It was Saturday and West Ham were playing Chelsea at Stamford Bridge. He wished the match had been at Upton Park. A lot of his mates had stopped travelling across London to Chelsea's ground. Funny, he thought, how the balance of "power" had shifted from East to West in a few years. He remembered when the Krays had been king-pins of violence in London and the East End had ruled the roost. Not now! Every section of the sprawling city had its claim to fame. South of the Thames the niggers rode cock-a-hoop in Brixton; the Irish held Shepherd's Bush with an iron fist; and the Jews predominated around Hampstead and Golders Green. The Cockney had lost control of his London. Even Soho had gone down the drain of provincial invasion. The pimps and touts there weren't old-established Londoner types. They came from Scouseland, Malta, Cyprus and Jamaica. Even the porno shops were having their difficulties with the parasitic influx of outside talent.

Like most of his generation, Joe *knew* about these things. At one time, East Enders enjoyed a visit to Soho and mingling with the "heavy boys" from Poplar and Plaistow and Barking. No longer. The word had circulated – stay away from Soho. Look for your heroes in Ilford, Forest Gate and Whitechapel. The old cockney thug was slowly being confined – to Bow, Mile End, Bethnal Green and their fringe areas. London was wide open now. To anyone with a gun, a cosh, an army of thugs.

Joe was brash enough to venture forth into enemy territory. He had seven mates – all tooled for trouble; all asking the same question: "Any aggro today?"

Slipping a light-weight cotton jacket over his gear, Joe studied himself in the mirror. The cosh didn't show under the jacket. He fingered his West Ham scarf, then threw it back into his wardrobe. *That* would be asking for police inspection... and the last thing he wanted was having his cosh found before he had an opportunity to use it.

He wasn't a bad-looking youth. At sixteen, he gave the impression of being at least nineteen. He was tall for his age – five-eleven. He had filled out and, at a fleeting glance, many a young girl's heart would flutter when he appeared on the scene. But his eyes could have deterred those females wary of sadistic companions. There was something in his gaze that spoke of brutality and nonconformity expressed in terms of physical rejection and explosive reaction.

At last, he was ready. Taking a final glance at his appearance, he nodded to his image, grinning approval. Then, with heavy boots making a resounding noise on the worn stair-carpet, he went to the front door, yelled: "I'm goin'," And left.

Outside, on the street, he paused.

God, how he hated this street! Next door, he could see that bitch Grace peeping from behind her curtains. What a bloody bitch she was! No matter how he acted, nor what he thought, he hated her for the way she had treated her husband. In a way, though, he was afraid of Grace. In his opinion, she was a black witch – and he didn't want to associate with her!

He hurried down the street, conscious of eyes following him. It was always the same. No matter how early he left the house, eyes always followed him. Sometimes he wondered if they ever slept in his dirty street.

He was whistling when he strolled down to the Barking Road. The cosh felt comfortable against his flesh. His boots felt solid, secure on his feet. In a few minutes he would meet his mates and, soon, they would be ready for aggro...

CHAPTER TWO

FRESH AIR in the pub was more valuable than gold dust. Smoke from countless pipes and smouldering cigarettes filled both bars, effectively helping to dull the clinging smell of cheap disinfectant. Nobody had ever asked the guvnor to list his establishment as a must on a tourist itinerary. It was unlikely anyone ever would.

If air was precious, a sentence spoken without four-letter emphasis was enough to bring sudden silence, raised eyebrows and get the speaker an award for bravery in the face of obscenity. Even the two barmaids spoke in anatomical descriptiveness and some of their suggestions were physical impossibilities except for a mechanical engineer.

His mates had the Saturday corner table and Joe shoved through the crowd, catching sight of Henry Downy at the bar. "Pint, mate," he yelled, getting a nod from the pimpled youth. Frankly, he couldn't stand the sight of Henry. The guy's pimples wanted to make him throw-up. Not just that, though – he had serious doubts about Henry's usefulness to the mob. He had always kept a close eye on Henry's activities and never ever gave advance information of an aggro when Henry was listening.

"You tooled?" Billy Endine asked nervously as he took his chair.

"Of course," Joe replied with an indignant sneer. "Think I'd go to fuckin' Chelsea without this?" His hand fondled the cosh under his shirt.

Billy shrugged and watched Henry struggle through the crowd with their beer. None of the boys tried to help the pimpled youth. It wasn't part of being mates to offer a helping hand. Not in their mob, anyway. "'Enery ain't got 'is!"

Joe fixed Henry with a malicious eye. He watched how the beer slopped on the table as the other nervously set it before him. "Wot's this about you not 'aving a tool?"

Henry glanced over his shoulder then spoke in a whisper. "My old man found it. Jeeze, didn't 'e raise hell!"

"You're a bleedin' liar, mate," Joe said deliberately. "Go get a tool or forget the game." His hand closed possessively round the glass, his mocking smile destroying Henry's unspoken reply in advance. As the pimple-face youth walked dejectedly away, Joe laughed. "Serves the bastard right! Drink up lads... 'is beer is good!"

From behind the bar, Mary Sommers watched the group. She couldn't take her gaze off Billy and, she felt sure, he was returning her interest each time he glanced across the pub. She was nearly old enough to be his mother but it didn't stop her having physical yearnings for him. It hadn't made her say no two weeks previously when Billy accosted her after closing. Nor had she tried to get away when he seemed to tire of feeling her. In fact, she could admit to herself that it was her prompting that had seen their confrontation develop into a frantic mating behind the soaring Point flats.

She knew she was asking for trouble getting involved with one of them yet her knees shook when she thought about how wonderful it had been pressed against his hard young body. Looking at Joe and the others she even wished Billy would waylay her tonight and share her with his mates. The escapade with Billy had opened floodgates inside her; made her realise how tame the past ten years had been with a man who really never gave sex a thought. She could remember when she was eighteen. Her proud boast then had been "I've been screwed by every man in the district". Since her marriage, she'd had about six bits on the side – hardly enough for a healthy, passionate woman with her shape.

Bending to pour a pint, she became aware of eyes peering down her wide-fronted blouse. She looked up, and caught the old lecher leaning forward to see more of her breasts. He turned away, smiling secretly. He'd had his eyeful and that was his fair share. At seventy-three a man could look but not touch.

Mary shrugged, her breasts jiggling firmly. The motion did not go un-noted. Those closest to the bar grinned; those at tables tried to catch her act but she refused to co-operate, her attention still rivetted on Billy and his mates.

"You don't want little bastards like them, Mary-girl!"

She swung on the man. "Mind your own fuckin' business," she snapped.

The man frowned. "Christ, lads – she's really after Joe!"

Let them get it wrong, Mary thought, flouncing down the bar. They'll be trying to catch me with Roy's son and I'll be rubbing against Billy. *God,* she sighed. *I wish I was!*

"That old cow!" Billy snorted disgustedly. "I jumped her an' she raped *me.*"

Joe twisted round, studying Mary with a lascivious eye. He had to admit she looked pretty good for a tart. Turning to Billy he grinned. "Was it good?"

"I've had worse."

"Arrange to meet her and we'll all be there..."

Billy frowned. "If she hollers, Joe..."

"Bloody hell, she's only a wet-knickered bitch! She won't holler. Go ahead – talk to her."

Billy got to his feet looking dubious. It was one thing trying to get a bit in the dark for yourself, he thought, but letting Joe and his other mates share – well, that was asking for big trouble. Since hanging had been abolished some magistrates were getting bleeding horrible with the amount of porridge they handed out. Especially when it involved tear-aways and girls! Bloody M.P.s, he thought. They got elected to do what their constituents wanted done and the bastards thought they were little tin-gods better than the voters! If he had his way every politician would be slung into prison and given a taste of what they deserved.

"Hey, Mary..." He leant against the bar between two huge coloured men. The stink of the blacks made him sick. He hated spades – wished they'd wash more often or get the hell back where they came from. This was *his* London – not somewhere for London Transport's African troops to live. He enjoyed the occasional aggro in Brixton. Smashing a few wog heads open always gave him greater satisfaction than bashing those bleeding Chelsea supporters.

Mary slopped beer into a glass and pushed it at her customer. She felt her knees go rubbery. Collecting the cash, she rang it up, then hurried along the bar to face Billy. Her eyes sparkled, her breasts heaved.

"Same again for the lads," Billy muttered, unable to tear his gaze from those beauties. It wasn't his round yet he couldn't come right out with the proposition. Joe's insistence on making Mary made him think about the other night and he suddenly realised how good it had been. Why should he share her with his mates?

"Billy wants to see you again, Mary..."

Billy glowered at Joe standing beside him now. Mary didn't flinch. She stared at Joe, asked softly, "Will you be there too?"

Joe nodded.

"When, Billy?"

The boy was lost. He couldn't understand a woman like her. He'd had his share of the little bits hanging around the fringes of their mob – the local girls trying to snare one of the better-known heroes. He'd even gone to bed with a Soho brass when they'd pulled a job off. But that had been a big disappointment. He'd felt sick, feeling around a professional tart.

"Tonight... when you finish here?" Joe asked.

Mary felt her throat constrict. She glanced up and down the bar. "Wait for me behind the Point?"

"We'll be there – won't we, Billy?"

Billy wanted to object. Knowing Joe, the woman would be subjected to extremes of intercourse before he – or any of the others – got their share. Yet, nobody denied Joe Hawkins his glory. "Yeah, Joe, that's fine."

Mary lowered her voice. "Forget this round – it's on me."

Joe laughed, returning to his seat. Mary would fiddle it. They were getting free beer on the guvnor for promising to give her what all concerned would thoroughly enjoy – especially Mary. The round was on her and everything else pleasurable would be on her, too.

The coloured man beside Billy laughed throatily, slapped Billy's shoulder. "Man, you'se got it made," he grinned.

Billy brushed the hand away and glared at the man. "Don't ever touch me, spade!" He backed away, ready to grab his tool.

Quickly, the two coloured men stiffened and moved to close in on their opponent. Then, suddenly – as the pub grew deathly silent – they glanced around and relaxed with foolish grins on their ebony faces. Even they had heard about Joe Hawkins, and his mob.

"Trouble, Billy?" Joe asked eagerly, watching the coloured men with what amounted to hungry appreciation. Like most East End skinheads – and, for that matter, population – Joe detested the influx of immigrants into what had always been a pure Cockney stronghold. It wasn't so much the colour of the skins that annoyed him. Any intruder would have been subject to the same treatment – be the man South African, Canadian, American. The East End was proud of its London-heritage; afraid to lose its ancient right to control what was, essentially, a Saxon bastion. 'Anglo-' had never been acceptable here. Loyalty to an established, accredited Cockney crown was taken for granted. In time of war, the East Ender had only to enter a recruiting office to be accepted as a fit example of a British fighting man. Nobody dare question that. Nor the right an East Ender had to voice his opinion regardless of Race Relations Board and governmental sympathies. Spades or wogs didn't count. They were impositions on the face of a London that should always be white, Cockney, true-British... not so-called British because they claimed a passport and insisted on rights their independent nations did not grant to the inhabitants of the British Isles.

"No trouble, man," the first immigrant said.

"None," his fellow black murmured.

Joe grinned evilly. He wasn't satisfied to let it go at that. This was Saturday – a day for splitting skulls. What better warm-up than these two coons...

"Apologize..." he suggested antagonistically, moving forward with his mob stepping in tight like a gang of Nazi S.S. men about to interrogate a prisoner.

Billy grinned. He felt tall, more than equal to a couple of hefty niggers now he had the backing of Joe and the lads. "Tell me how sorry you fuckin' well are," he snarled.

The first negro blanched. He lived in Plaistow and knew how difficult it could be to oppose this gang of young thugs. He had heard of other immigrants whose homes had been terrorized. He had been warned by the pastor not to invite racial discontent with the 'ignorant' Londoner. Mentally, he rejected these white savages – and all Englishmen – as inferiors striving to prove their right to subjugate black peoples. He didn't stop to think about the poverty and superstition that made his homeland a place to avoid, or leave, nor the debt each of his people owed to the British administrators, the British tax-payer, the British sense of fair-play. He forgot these things because he wanted a job, a decent home – even if, after occupation, he turned it into a slum-dwelling – and a right to stand on his own feet without having a witch-doctor, a tribal chieftain, or an arrogant headman telling him what to do, when to do it, how to do it. He remembered his rights in England – the right to protest and call the British bastards and exploiters.

"I'se sorry, *boss*," he snarled.

Joe laughed. "Boss? Sambo – get stuffed!" He turned away in disgust. The Chelsea mob would offer more resistance.

Billy puffed out his skinny chest and pushed past the coloured men.

Conversation started again in the pub and Mary's eyes glittered frantically as she kept watching Joe, Billy and the mob. These were her type of men, she thought. She loathed serving blacks. She detested their lecherous looks, their arrogant attempts to strip her across the bar and the almost "don't dare refuse me" propositions they made. But the guvnor had warned her not to invite trouble by refusing to serve them.